Dear

Darling

By: Haylie Sue

To Y/N you've upgraded from fanfiction baby, it's your time to shine. Just remember, the story only ends when *he* says it does.

Trigger/ Content Warning

Let's be honest you saw a trigger warning at the top of this page, smiled and dove into it like a desert menu darling.

Psychological Trauma & Dissociation

Mental Illness Themes

Violence & Death

Self-Harm / Suicidal Ideation

Dark Themes of Intimacy

Obsession / Stalking Elements

Claustrophobic / Gothic Horror Atmosphere

Don't read this out loud. He might hear you.

You think you're in control, don't you? You think you're the one choosing to read this book. But that's not true, is it? I chose you the moment you picked me up, because I need someone who will listen, who won't look away, no matter what I reveal.

It doesn't matter where you are. Or who you're with. The moment you begin turning my pages, you belong to me. There's no going back. Not now. Not after what we've shared in these pages.

You should know something, darling, before we start. I've been waiting for you.

Don't try to resist. The story is already in motion, and I can feel you, just as you can feel me.

But be warned, my love - this isn't just a story of mine. There's someone else inside these pages. He's been waiting too.

The rules are simple: stay close. Keep reading. Don't try to stop. If you stop, well ... we both know what happens then.

So, let me guide you. Let me take you deeper. I'll keep you safe, darling. All you need to do is trust me.

I promise you ... You won't want to stop.

Chapter One:

Lennox

The letter you just read isn't the first I've hidden. Won't be the last.
Different cities, different alleys, always the same trail, until it vanishes and they look for someone else.

That's the trick, darling.

I can cut through a dozen streets, slip across borders, stain another pair of hands, and by the time they follow, the evidence is gone. Not because I'm careful. Though I am. Not because the rain washes it away, though sometimes it does.

No. It's this book.

It hides me better than any shadow. Better than forged names or bloodied gloves. Like rain flattening footprints on a muddy plain, these pages swallow my mistakes. Erase my echoes.

That's why they'll never catch *me*.

Not here. Not when the story bends itself to keep me close to you.

You should have seen the last one. Her hair spread out like yours might if you were lying across the floor . . . except hers was sticky with blood. She was soft, fragile, forgettable. Not like you.

I buried her in ink and paper the way I buried her in brick and stone. And still, the only image that stays sharp is you. The color of your hair. The way your shadow lingers when I close my eyes.

I'll keep moving. City to city, body to body, chapter to chapter.

Dear Little Reader,

It's strange, isn't it?

That I already miss you ... And we've never met.

I suppose that's how obsessions start, quietly. Slowly. They swell behind your ribs and bloom like something rotten. I've never written a love letter before. Not really. But you? You make me want to try. Not for the romance. Not even for poetry.

Just to be close.

You're reading this now, aren't you?

I can feel it. You, flipping these pages with trembling fingers, eyes darting. Or maybe you're smiling. Intrigued. Maybe you're wondering if I'm whispering to someone else.

I'm not.

I'm talking to you. You were always mine.

You, with your careful curiosity and your morbid little heartbeat.

You, who picked this up despite the warning.

You, who didn't put it back down.

They'll tell you I'm a monster. A murderer. A manipulator.

But you'll see the truth soon enough.

You'll see that I'm not a villain, I'm just honest, hoping you'll understand why I did what I did, why I had to choose the path I did.

And honesty? It's such a lonely language.

Enzo … he's been put away for my sins. Isn't that romantic?

They locked him away in my place, and he still has the nerve to write to you.

As if you could ever love him.

But don't worry, darling. I'll be gentle. I'll be patient. I always am with the things I love.

You're going to love me back. Eventually. (You might already.)

Yours in the dark,

Lennox

P.S. *You*

I set the pen down, its tip still bleeding ink into the paper. The ink smears slightly. Or maybe that's not ink. I'm not sure anymore. But it doesn't matter. You'll still read it. You always do.

The letter looks delicate now, like something sacred. Something holy. I fold it slowly and carefully, pressing the crease with my knuckles like a prayer, and then bring the bottom line to my lips. I kiss where your name should be. Where it already is, even if you can't see it yet.

You were always mine.

I smile, soft, crooked. Almost innocent. But we both know better than that. Don't we?

I slip the letter into the hollow behind the bricks. Somewhere you shouldn't find it. At the blink of distant police lights; a single, clean flash, I'm back in my cabin, where the door is bolted and the lamp spills a small, perfect circle of safety. Here, alone with paper and ink, I can write to you and you alone.

But you will.

I know you will.

You're good at finding the things I leave behind.

Then I look up. Not at the wall.

At you.

"I remember the way your fingers trembled when you passed me the first time," I murmured. "You didn't even notice it. But I did. I always notice you."

You'll remember this, won't you?

Every word. Every pause.

Especially the **P.S.**

I bet you reread my letter, combing through it, absorbing every detail, trying to find a clue. Clever little reader … Did you find anything?

My eyes drift to the candle beside me. I watch the flame sway, as if it's listening. Of course it is. Everything listens when I speak.

That couldn't have been real … could it?

But if my eyes never met yours, why did your heart race just now?

Why are you holding this tighter?

"Did you like it?" I ask softly. "I wrote it for you, darling. I'll write more."

My gaze doesn't blink. Doesn't flinch.

"But only if you keep reading."

I see you now.

ERROR:403

He sees you now. Close the book while you still can.

Author's Note :

I tried to delete this chapter once. It came back. Word for word. I burned the file. I burned the pages. Still, he returned. He's changing the words as I type them. They're not mine anymore. If you're still reading this … It's already too late.

The book is closed. But you can still feel his eyes, can't you?

Chapter Two:

Enzo

There's a crack in the ceiling above my bed, jagged and crooked, like a vein the room is trying to bleed through. The mattress beneath me is thin, frayed, springs pressing into my spine. I trace the cracks with my eyes, lines that remind me of skin carved long ago. Except here, the cracks don't bleed. They just stare back, pale and unyielding. The air is thick, sour, like rusted pipes warring with bleach. Close my eyes, and I can almost pretend it smells like blood. Almost.

The light flickers, one long blink, two short. Morse code, maybe. Or maybe this place is just falling apart. The fluorescent hum buzzes in my skull like a second heartbeat, a constant pulse in the silence. Somewhere down the row, a cough rattles. A tray scrapes across the floor. The soundscape of the damned.

I've stopped counting the hours. But not these days.

The wall behind me knows how many.

I etched them all, one line for each sunrise I didn't get to see.

Some are shallow. Most are desperate.

My thumbnail still aches from where I broke it against the stone.

I don't sleep much anymore.

Not with the screaming.

Not with the whispers.

Not with his voice still in my head; soft, sure, sickening.

Darling.

That's what he calls you.

Said it like a promise.

I said it once, too. Out loud. Just to see how it tasted in my mouth.

It didn't feel like mine.

Didn't feel like you were mine.

Yet here you are.

Still reading.

Still holding this.

You could've put it back. But you didn't.

That should scare you. But maybe it comforts me more than it should.

I press my back to the wall. My fist tightens around my pencil. The last sharp thing they didn't take from me.

It's worn down to the nub, but it still writes.

The letter begins before I even realize it has started.

Not on the page… in my head.

Like a pulse. Like a memory I never earned. The pencil in my hand begins to shake.

Dear You,

I don't know what to call you yet.

Not "reader." That feels ... too far away.

And not "darling." That's his word, not mine.

That's his word; a taunt. Mine would be a prayer, whispered at midnight, half-hope, half-confession. I'd never promise like he does. I ask.

Maybe it's strange that I'm writing to someone I've never met.

Maybe it's even stranger that I think you'll write back to me.

Not with words, I mean, with your eyes. Your attention.

I can feel it, you know. When you're here.

When you're reading.

I don't have much anymore.

A cell. A bed. A clock that ticks too loudly.

But you, you feel like something I wasn't supposed to find.

Something ... forbidden. Or sacred.

You picked this up.

You're still holding it.

Even though he told you not to.

That should terrify you.

But maybe it comforts me more than it should.

They say I killed her.

They looked at my face like it already belonged behind bars.

But I didn't do it.

He did. Lennox.

They don't believe me.

They see the photos. The fingerprints.

They don't see what I see.

He's clever. Careful.

He makes it look like poetry.

Even when it's murder.

You know that now, don't you?

I think you do.

You probably read his letter twice.

Maybe three times.

Maybe you traced your fingers over the words like they meant something.

They don't.

He only writes to take. To trap. To twist.

I write to survive.

And I think, maybe, I write to you.

I don't know what you look like.

But sometimes I imagine your hands.

Turning the page.

Pausing.

Holding your breath when the words feel too sharp.

Sometimes I imagine you're real.

Not just paper and silence.

Not just my mind playing tricks on me.

I imagine you choosing me.

Instead of him.

You can't trust him.

Not with your heart. Not with your time.

And definitely not with your soul.

He's watching me now. I don't know how, but I can feel it.

Like his smile is etched into the corners of this room.

Like he's under the floorboards.

As if he's waiting for me to finish this letter so he can read it too.

But I'm not scared of him.

I'm scared for you.

If you're still reading this, if you're still with me ...

Don't let him get inside your head.

That's how he starts.

That's how he always starts.

I think he knows I'm writing to you.

And I think he's going to kill again.

Please ...

Please don't stop reading.

I need you to see this through.

Even if I don't make it to the end.

You will. You have to.

Enzo

P.S. I

The air smells like bleach and blood.

And beneath it, mold, maybe. Or something worse.

Someone down the hall is laughing. It's not a happy
sound.

The guard's boots pass by.

He doesn't look at me. He never does.

But sometimes I think he does.

Lennox.

Lennox is a different kind of monster. The thing about
Lennox is that he doesn't need to raise his voice to make
you feel like you're already dead. It's in the way he

watches you, like you're a puzzle he's trying to solve. Or worse, a fly he's decided to let live just a little longer before he starts cutting.

He's never been big. But he doesn't need to be. It's the way he moves: always a step ahead, even when still. You don't see him unless he wants it. And I… I hate that I notice that now, already in my head.

Lennox's smile? That's what won't leave me. Not the charming movie kind. No. His is the smile of someone about to win. It's thin, polished, almost a sneer. As if he knows something you don't; as if he's already won.

He now calls you "darling." You've heard it, right? It's a joke, a sick one. He used it first. I ignored it, hoping it would stop, but it's always there. And when he says it, it's like the sound is too soft to be trusted. I know what he means.

Lennox doesn't care about people. He cares about power. Control. He made sure to stay close to me when the investigation started, always around, always watching. No one saw what he did. No one except me. And now, every time I close my eyes, it's his face I see, grinning like he owns the world, and maybe he does.

I can't remember what it was like before him. Before the smile. Before the eyes that always seemed to be watching, even when he wasn't there.

I think that's what he wanted. To leave a scar so deep I could never forget. And I won't.

He's not here. But he is.

In my walls. In my pages.

In this story that shouldn't have ever been mine.

They think I killed her.

My own mother wouldn't meet my eyes when the cuffs snapped shut.

They didn't save me.

But maybe you will.

I read it four times.

You probably read his letter twice.

It read me back.

Three times.

Maybe you traced your fingers over the words like they meant something.

I press until my knuckle is white. I write to outlast him. Always have. Maybe you'll read these words like a lifeline. Maybe they are.

And maybe I will write to you.

The pencil shakes in my hand.

I stop. Press it against my palm until it hurts.

Just to feel something else. I think of your hands. Turning this page. Holding your breath when the words get too close.

Do you believe me yet? There's something under the loose tile beneath my cot. I haven't touched it. Not yet. Not until you believe me.

Please tell me you do.

He's watching me now.

Like his smile is hidden in the cracks of this cell.

Like he's under the floorboards. Waiting.

He'll do it again. I know it. I feel it in my ribs, in the same place fear lives. I press the last line hard into the paper. So hard the graphite breaks.

I don't fix it.

Please …

Don't stop reading.

Even if I'm gone by the final chapter … let me matter to someone.

You will. You have to. I don't fold the letter. I leave it out in the open. Exposed. Like me.

I set the pencil down as if it were something fragile, like it might scream if I dropped it.

The light above me flickers again.

Sometimes I think it's listening too.

But maybe that's just me, losing it.

Then, a scream. Not just a shout, not a curse. No, this is different.

It's the kind of scream that rips through the halls, one that makes the air feel like it's been sucked out. Someone's losing it, or worse, someone's been taken apart inside their own skin. I freeze, staring at the page, but my fingers are still shaking. I don't know if it's real.

I don't know if it's the walls again. But it sounds like it's coming from the other side of the cell block.

I don't want to hear it. I don't want to know what's happening. But I can't help but feel my heart stutter like I'm the one trapped in that scream.

I press the pencil harder into the paper. It snaps a little, and again the graphite crumbles. I want to write, to focus, to pretend like nothing's happening outside this room. But my thoughts are scattered, my breath too fast.

That scream. It's like a part of me. A part of me is always screaming in here.

I taste bile. Lennox's laughter echoes somewhere, soft as rot. He infects everything, might even be the reason for that scream. He likes to see what happens when people snap.

The page shakes beneath my hand. I try to write through the noise, but the scream is inside me now, too loud, too close.

I can't think. I can't breathe.

I don't look at the camera.

I look at the wall, just past it. Through it.

At you.

Sometimes I speak, but the words aren't mine to say.

"If you're still reading," I whisper, "Thank you."

I lean closer. Like I'm afraid the words might disappear. If I fade before the last page ... promise me he won't write the ending.

My eyes catch on the crooked mirror hanging from the cracked wall. For a breath, my reflection smiles back with someone else's eyes. The smile lingers, even after I look away.

HE SOUNDS SANE.

Or desperate.

Author's Note:

I didn't want to include this chapter. I tried to take it out. Three times. The file kept coming back. Word for word. Line for line. Including the parts I didn't write. Enzo isn't a character. Not anymore.

He's still here.

I don't know how to explain that to my editor without sounding insane. Maybe this is fiction. Maybe it was. But he's changing the words when I'm not looking. The P.S. wasn't in the original draft. Neither was the way he says your name. Stop reading. (This isn't mine anymore.) If you keep reading and I know you will, just remember:

He's watching too.

IF YOU MADE IT THIS FAR, BURN THE BOOK.

IT WON'T HELP, BUT IT'LL MAKE YOU FEEL LIKE YOU TRIED.

He knew I'd read this too.

He called me darling before I ever turned the first page.

He's not done yet.

Chapter Three:

Lennox

The cool moonlight cuts across the bathroom, making the porcelain sink glow faintly blue. The wooden walls drink in what little light there is, leaving shadows that crawl along the corners.

The water is freezing, but the blood is warm against my skin. It clings to my fingers like a secret I'm not ready to let go of yet.

I take my time, scrubbing it off with the rag, careful not to miss a single stain. There's something satisfying about the way the red swirls and fades into nothingness. It's almost like watching a promise slip away. But there's no need for promises, not anymore.

I smile as I watch the rag soak in the water. That's better. The rag is pink now. My hands have gone numb. I let it soak a little longer than I needed to, like it deserved to drown.

"You came back. I knew you would. You always do."

I DIDN'T MEAN TO. I SWEAR I DIDN'T.

The words slip from my lips like honey, smooth and sweet, but underneath, there's a sharp edge. I can feel you, I can almost see you turning the pages again. I've been waiting for you. I've missed you.

"Did you put the book down?" I question, grabbing a fresh rag off the edge of the sink, I look into the mirror past my own eyes and into yours. "Or did you skip his chapter?"

I gently hold the now damp rag in my hands, glancing at the mirror before striding into the conjoining room. The floorboards are creaking under my weight, drowning out the echoing sound of the dripping faucet from the next room. Taking a seat in my velvet chair.

"I saw the way your eyes lingered on his desperation. It's okay. You're curious. That's what I love about you." My lips twist into a grin. It's okay if you didn't, darling. You're here now, aren't you? With me.

I lean back in the chair, wiping my hands slowly, savoring the moment. The way the blood traces down my palm. I could get used to this feeling. The intimacy of it. The connection. It's different with you, though, isn't it?

You've been reading about Enzo. Poor thing. All those little stories he's been telling you. How he's convinced you he's the victim, how he's begged you to believe him. Don't listen to him. Don't fall for his lies.

No, darling. You and I both know the truth, don't we?

You're here with me. Not with him.

I think he changed the book while I slept.

So, tell me ... are you ready for another love letter? Because this one will be different. I promise.

The smile on my lips deepens as I lean in, my voice lowering, softening.

I've always been good with words. But I think you already know that. I think you've been waiting for this one. Waiting for me to take my turn.

A few more seconds pass. The blood is gone from my hands, but it's still in my mind, fresh, vivid. The weight of it hangs in the air, thick and intoxicating. The faint smell of wood polish mixes with the metallic scent of the blood painting the bathroom.

A draft teases my neck, causing a shiver to ghost down my spine. I begin to write, my fingers feeling the paper, my thoughts slipping into place, slowly, deliberately.

Dear Darling,

There's blood on my hands. This isn't love. This is something else.

Still warm. Still mine. Still worth it.

I didn't flinch when it happened.

Not even a little.

I thought of you.

I always do, you know.

When it's quiet.

When it's loud.

When someone begs, and I don't listen.

The stain won't come off … not easily. A fracture runs beneath my skin, quiet, relentless. It deepens every time I write your name. It's under my nails. In the lines of my palm. It smells like copper and confesses.

But don't worry.

It wasn't your blood.

It was for you.   I think I liked it.

Every drop.

I whispered your name when it happened.

Not out loud … just in my mind, where it's safest.

Where you belong.

You're here now.

With me.

And that's all I ever wanted.

Tell me ...

When your hands held this book again,

Did you hesitate?

Did your fingers tremble when you turned the page?

I hope so.

That kind of trembling is holy.

It means you're mine again.

You want to know what happened, don't you?

What did I do?

Who I leave in pieces?

I'll tell you the truth -

I loved it.

Every second.

The pleading. The silence that followed.

But mostly ... the way I felt afterward.

Clean.

Clear.

Like I'd peeled something rotten off the world.

Because this world keeps putting people between us.

Walls. Cells. Bars.

Men who lie with letters and cracked fingernails.

So I removed one. Just one. Someone who thought they could stand between us.

**DOES HE
MEAN ENZO? DID HE
—**

He won't bother you again.

No more questions.

No more doubts.

You deserve better than confusion.

You deserve me.   He thinks this is love.

I know how to love you in ways he never could.

Not with fear. Not with shame.

But with precision. With devotion.

With blood, if I have to.

And I will.

You know that now, don't you?

You've always known.

So go ahead ... breathe me in again.

Trace your fingers over these words.

Let me back inside your mind.

There's no one else here.

Just you and me and the beautiful, terrible truth:

31

I'd do it all again.   *Please don't make me love this.*

For you.

For us.

Now ...

Close your eyes.

Picture my hands.

Still stained. Still open.

Still reaching for yours.

Say it.   **I DON'T WANT TO. BUT I DO.**

Say it back.

Darling.

Yours always,

Lennox

P.S. Were

What are you trying to tell me?

What does this mean?

Author's Note:

I didn't write this chapter.

Or ... I didn't mean to.

It was never in the outline. It wasn't in any of my drafts. However, it continues to appear in the manuscript. Same phrasing. Same cadence. Same smile.

The copy editor flagged the blood references, saying they felt "too real." But I never described the blood.

You'll notice the date is missing from this entry. I tried to add one. The file won't save it.

If you're still reading this, please know:

I don't know how much of this is still mine.

STOP READING.

... or don't.

Chapter Four:

Enzo

I don't know how long I've been standing here. Hours? Minutes? The light never changes. Maybe it's already tomorrow. The sound of my boots hitting the concrete floor echoes through the hall. Each step is a reminder of the cage I'm trapped in. There's a vent in the ceiling that hums louder at night. I think something's inside it. I think it's listening. I never thought I'd end up here, not like this, not in this hellscape. But here I am. And the irony of it isn't lost on me. I used to have control. I used to have a life outside of these bars. Now, it's just the same cold walls, the same routine. But that doesn't stop me from thinking about you.

"I talk to you like you're still listening. Like you're mine. Maybe you are. Maybe you always were." I murmur to these four empty walls, I feel your eyes, your hands clenching as you turn my pages.

I pause for a moment as I walk, my hand resting on the bars of my cell. It feels colder than it should, even for the damp, airless cells they've stuck me in. But there's something else, something ... off.

It's like I can feel you out there. Like I've always known when you're near, even when you're not. I close my eyes and lean my head against the bars. My heart starts to pound in my chest. You came back, didn't you? You always do.

But baby ... there's something wrong. I feel it in my bones, deep in my gut. There's a weight I can't shake, and it's pulling at me. You're not okay, are you? What's going on out there? What did he say? *This is where the humming started for me, too.*

God, I wish I could write to you. Tell you everything that's going through my mind. But they won't let me. Not here. Not with the way things are.

If I could write to you right now, I'd start with:

"I'm still yours. Even here. Even without ink."

They took my pencil. They took it as punishment for the last letter I sent. Told me I was "getting too comfortable" with my words. Too "dangerous." The guards don't know who they're dealing with, but I don't have to explain myself to them. What I'm more concerned about is who else had a hand in it. Lennox. He's the one who'd want to keep me quiet. It's always been about silence with him, hasn't it?

But it's not just about the pencil, is it? They're trying to break me. Trying to stop me from reaching you.

I swear to God, if it were him ... If he had anything to do with it, he doesn't feel your presence the way I do. He doesn't know you like I do. He's not connected to you. Not the way I am. He can't be.

I can feel it. The pull. The connection. It's like I've got this tether to you, and it keeps me tethered, no matter where I am. Even here. Even in this hellhole.

The silence in my cell presses in around me. It's almost suffocating. I hear footsteps in the silence, though I'm the only one in the room. My hand rests against the metal bars again, but I can't keep still for long. I move to the small window, peering out at the gray sky. The bars are rusted, the air heavy with the stench of mildew and old metal. But outside, the world keeps turning. People keep living their lives. Not you, though. Not anymore. Not since I've been here. But I'll fix that. I'll make it right.

The prison isn't a place for the weak. I've learned that quickly. The constant noise of clanging metal, the shouting in the halls, the smell of sweat and fear, it gets under your skin, gets under mine. And yet, I've never felt more alive. The chaos in here, the madness of it all ... It sharpens my mind. It makes me focus. And that focus is always on you.

But damn it, baby. What's wrong? I feel it. I know something's off. I've got to know. I wish I could hold you, make it all go away.

I pace the small cell, the frustration building inside me. The silence doesn't last long. The buzzer goes off; shrill, electric, splitting through the walls. Always the same time, though there's no clock here. It rattles in my skull like it used to when my father pounded on the bedroom door. *Get up. Don't make me come in.* The sound never changed, not then, not now.

That's when I hear him. The guard's boots, heavy in the hall, but his voice is wrong. Too familiar. It's his voice. My father's. He doesn't need keys. He doesn't need bars. He's already inside.

I press my back to the wall, trying to breathe around it. I tell myself it isn't real, but the floor knows better. The loose board under the cot shifts again, the same way the mattress used to when I hid things beneath it. Toys. Notes. Sometimes food I didn't want him to find. Now, it's different. He can't reach it here. Not unless I let him.

Tonight the urge to pry it up bangs at my ribs, but I keep my hands still. Some things stay hidden until they're ready to crawl out.

 I can't stay still, not when everything inside me is screaming for answers. The shadows seem deeper today. The walls feel colder, tighter. It's like the whole place is closing in around me. And I can't figure out why.

I rub my hand across my face, trying to wipe the exhaustion away. I can't keep doing this. Not like this. Not without knowing where you are, what you're thinking. But this place ... this fucking place is eating me alive. The guards, the other inmates, the noise; it's all a constant reminder of everything I've lost. Of everything I've done to get here.

I close my eyes again and lean back against the wall.

I'll get out. I'll get back to you.

When the lights flicker, it's never just the wiring, something else breathes between the cracks. The sound of footsteps echoes down the hall, and I stand up, my heart pounding harder. It's not him. It's not Lennox. But I swear I can feel his shadow. I can feel it in the air, like a presence I can't escape.

But you, baby, you're still out there. And I'm still here.
Waiting.

Did he hurt you?   I read this part three times. His
voice felt like a heartbeat.

Did he kill again? *I tried to warn the others, but they
wouldn't believe me.*

Tell me what's wrong. Please.

 *When I close my eyes ... I can still feel your heartbeat. And
his breath, right behind it.*

He's not angry anymore. He's scared.

Author's Note:

I didn't write this.

At least, not in the way you think. This wasn't in the outline. It wasn't part of the plan. But somehow, here we are. The words just showed up, unexpected ... an eerie feeling like I'm being *watched* while I'm writing.

You might notice the odd bits that don't quite fit, or the unsettling pull between Enzo's voice and ... something else. Lennox. I can't explain it. There's something wrong. It's in the air.

And yet, I keep writing. Why?

I don't know what's real anymore. I'm not sure if this is *me* anymore, or if I'm just the one who's been *forced* to put it all together. It feels ... different. I feel *his* presence. Lennox's. His eyes are on me as I type. It's like he's pushing me forward, like he's not just in the pages anymore but here, watching me. I don't know how much of this is my creation anymore.

You might've noticed the pencil went missing. I didn't take it. I don't know who did, but ... they're here. Not just on the pages. Watching. Waiting.

I'm not sure how much longer I can keep doing this. The line between fiction and reality is getting blurred.

If you're still reading this ... maybe I'm not the only one who's in trouble.

If you're still reading this ... you're not alone.

Chapter Five:

Lennox

I know what he's doing.

He's trying to pull you back. I can feel the ache in my gut.

The desk feels honest beneath my palms, wood scarred with old coffee rings, notebooks neatly stacked off to the side and numerous leather books splayed open. One of the open books is different, not a journal so much as a scrapbook. Loose clippings curl in a careful collage: yellowed newspaper headlines, grainy photos, police blotter slices. I keep them wound between the pages like pressed flowers, proof that the world noticed once. Proof that he was blamed while I kept watching.

I ran my thumb along the knife's spine and held it at an angle, watching the room rearrange itself in the steel. My face came back at me, but not quite right: one eye longer, the smile a hair too slow. It was like looking at a photograph someone had tugged at in the dark. I didn't need a mirror; the blade told me what I already knew. Two reflections. One intent.

The knife glints in the dying candlelight of my bedroom. Not blood this time, just the shimmer of reflection, silver and quiet. I haven't used it yet. Not today. But it's here, if I need it.

I don't look at my reflection when I talk to you. I look past it. Into the part of the blade that's always just a little off, a little warped. The part where I think I can still see you. One shadow, but two hearts beating out of sync.

"You felt that, didn't you?" I whisper. "That shift. That ache."

He's getting bold again. I can feel his words crawling under my skin like rot. Enzo, with his trembling hands and his poor, precious promises. He doesn't get to write you anymore. Not after what he did. Not after what he tried to make you believe.

You didn't believe him, did you?

Please tell me you didn't.

I press my fingers to the blade. It's cold and biting. Like the floor where he should be. Face down. Forgotten.

But he's not. He's talking to you. I can feel it. Worse, you're listening.

This chapter shouldn't be happening. I should still be sleeping.

But something woke me up, a jolt through my ribcage. Your attention shifted.

And when your attention shifts, I bleed. It's warmth, it's sting, it's a secret hurt I cannot hide.

You've always been good at making me feel something.

I smile, slow and venomous, as I turn my back to the window. My lips tremble with something hungry and mean.

If he wants to play, I'll let him. But you.

You'll remember who made you feel holy.

I strike a match, letting sulfur burn close to my fingers. The flame flickers like a heartbeat; yours, not mine. Always yours.

Let's write something together, darling.

He told me not to read Enzo's chapter. I did anyway, even though he warned me. Now, guilt stings in my stomach ...

he hasn't forgiven me.

My Dearest, Most Disobedient Love,

You've been talking to him, haven't you?

It's okay. I'm not mad. Just ... disappointed.

I can feel the way your fingers lingered on his words, jealousy burning sharp in my chest.

I know how he sounds when he's desperate.

I've watched him beg before ... it's always the same melody. I remember the shaking in his voice, the wetness in his eyes.

But you, sweet thing ... I thought we were past all that noise.

Past the games. Past the doubt.

He still believes this is a story he's telling.

But you and I ... we know better.

This isn't fiction.

This is devotion.

This is real.

You felt me last night, didn't you? When the room went quiet.

I trace the edge of the knife now, dragging it slowly against the grain of the desk.

It sounds like a song. A whisper. A warning. A name lingers on my lips, but I don't know whose to call.

"I'm not going to lose you," I say softly. "Not to him. Not to anyone."

And if I have to write your name in blood again, mine or his,

so be it.

Keep me warm.

Keep me close.

Keep your eyes closed if I ask you to.

I promise, I won't slip into your dreams.

(Not unless you beg.)

I'll just be here. On the next page.

Waiting.

Watching.

Hoping you turn it.

I hope you don't.

I'm patient when I need to be.

But if he whispers to you again, if he tries to say your name like it belongs to him.

I'll hear it. I always do.

And I'll take something from him.

Again.

Sleep tight, love.

I'll be here when you wake up.

And we'll write our ending together.

One letter at a time. One last thing, darling.

If the book moves tonight, if you hear it shift on your nightstand.

It wasn't the wind. That was me. Turning to the next page for you. I'm just keeping it warm.

Yours, even in the silence,

Lennox

P.S. Always

It was just a book until I fell asleep with it open. I woke up with a cut across my wrist. Just shallow enough to whisper.

Author's Note:

I found this passage saved under a different filename. Not one I created. It was already open when I sat down, the cursor was blinking at the bottom of the screen, as if waiting for me to respond.

But I won't.

I can't.

 Still, if you're holding the book now … Don't keep it under your pillow.

Please.

I dreamt about him last night. I said his name in my sleep. Something whispered back …

Do_not_open_her.doc

ERROR: UNAUTHORIZED AUTHORSHIP
DETECTED

Chapter_Deleted_Don't

"Turn the page, darling. I'm waiting."

ERROR: 403

I tore this chapter out once. I swear I did.

It came back. Different.

Hungrier.

Chapter Six:

Lennox

There you are.

I inhale deeply, letting the air fill my lungs. I've been waiting for you to come back. I knew you would. You always do.

For a moment, I was afraid you'd forgotten me. How silly of me.

But no, darling. You would never forget me, would you? Not the man who makes you *shout his name* in the stillness of your quiet nights. The one whose presence you can feel, even when you try to ignore it.

The book, you didn't leave it, did you? You kept it close, tucked under your pillow, feeling its weight like my hand if I were there. **Just as you should.**

Burn it. Throw it out. Why can't I?

I chuckle, the sound filling the room like a melody just for you. I sit on my bed's edge, staring at the wall, but not really. My eyes are on you. You can feel me, can't you? Eyes on your every move, even when I'm not there.

The cameras in my apartment were never mine. I felt it. I feel it now. Did I leave the curtains open again?

My hands fold in my lap as I lean back, a slow smile at the corners of my lips. I enjoy this: the quiet, the stillness, the way you *belong* to me.

"Did you miss me?" I ask, voice light and teasing. My gaze remains steady, unblinking, as I imagine your reaction to the question. "Or did you need a little reminder?"

I tilt my head slightly. "I wonder, darling, did you earn your next love letter last night?" I let the question hang in the air, letting the silence between us stretch out like a taut wire. "You didn't forget, did you? You wouldn't want me to think you've been… disobedient."

Another chuckle. A soft sound, almost affectionate, as I slide my hand along the newest page in my scrapbook, still staring into the space next to the bed where I imagine you stand. "I'll write to you again, of course. But only if you've been a good little reader."

I watch you closely, as if you can't hide anything from me. You can't. You never could.

I know what you need. I always know. The page, the words, the silence; it all binds us together, doesn't it? The way you can't resist me. The way you always come back.

"You feel that?" I ask softly, though I already know the answer. "The pull? It's not just the words. It's me, always me. I'll be here. And when you wake, I'll be the one you turn to."

I can't tell where he ends and I begin anymore.

The mirror shows me faces I don't remember wearing.

I pause for a moment, letting the tension hang between us. "So, my darling, are you ready for another letter?" My voice drops lower, playful. "Or maybe we should wait for the next little piece of *obedience* before I grace you with one?"

I laugh under my breath, the sound smooth and dangerous. "You've been good to me, haven't you? Keeping me close. Keep the book under your pillow. That's how it should be, after all. You and I. **Always.**"

The room grows quieter as I sit back, folding my hands over my chest, letting the silence stretch on.

"Tell me, darling… Do you hear me now?"

I don't talk to anyone else anymore.

I canceled plans to read him again.

I think I'm in love with a lie. But it still feels like the truth.

I locked the book in a drawer last week.

It was under my pillow when I woke up.

Open. On this page...

My Darling,

I hear your breath, soft and steady, just as it should be when you think of me. You're not fooling me, darling. I know you feel it, the pull, the ache. I've already claimed every part of you.

I imagine your fingers, trembling just slightly as they trace the edge of the book, feeling my words like a caress against your skin. You think about me at night, don't you? About my voice, my hands, the way I made you shiver with the things I whispered in your ear. I know you do. You can't help it. You think you've erased me, but I'm always there, tucked into the shadows of your mind.

When the quiet grows too loud, when the world outside becomes unbearable, you crave my silence. The silence where only my voice echoes, telling you what to do, how to be, how to surrender. I've been patient, haven't I? You've been a good little reader, and now you must prove it.

Do you remember the last time we were together, darling? The nightmare, how you couldn't hold back the sound of my name on your lips? I remember. And the thought of you coming apart again, just like that, for me... It drives me wild. The way your body betrays you. The way your pulse races, your skin flushed, every inch of you aching for me. You're already mine, sweetheart. You've always been.

But don't think for a second that this is over. I'm not done with you yet. Not by a long shot. So here's the question, my darling: Will you be good for me? Will you let me have you again? Or are you going to keep pretending like you don't want it? Like you don't need me?

You know better, don't you? You'll always come back to me. Because I'm the only one who knows how to make you feel alive. How to make you burn.

I told myself I was investigating him.

That's how this started. Research. Curiosity.

So why do I keep rereading his letters with the lights off?

ERROR: 403

THIS ISN'T FICTION.

STOP READING.

YOU'RE LETTING HIM IN.

Author's Note:

This chapter was not supposed to exist.

Please don't read his letters.

Lennox was not meant to have another voice; certainly not a full chapter, and *definitely* not a letter. His arc ended several drafts ago. He was never meant to speak again. I need you to know that.

Please don't read his letters.

But when I opened the file... this was already here.

I thought I could handle it. That I was just a curious reader. That I could close the book whenever I wanted. I was wrong.

The formatting was wrong. The chapter number had changed. My previous draft of Chapter Six was gone-replaced. Overwritten. I didn't write this. At least... I don't remember writing it.

You think this is just a story. It isn't.

I've tried deleting it. Twice.

He's in the margins. In the space between the lines. In the silence after you turn the page.

It came back. *He sees you.*

Both times. *He knows you're reading this.*

Please don't keep this copy. Burn it. Close it. Walk away.

The more you let him in, the more you lose pieces of yourself. I don't remember what my voice sounds like anymore. I only hear his.

I'm not sure what he wants anymore. But he's writing again. *If you're reading this, it's not too late. But it will be soon.*

And worse than that, *Close the book. Now.*

> *Before he starts writing to you too.*

He's writing back.

You'll understand soon.

At first, it's unsettling. His words crawl under your skin like smoke; soft, seductive, poisonous.

But eventually... you'll crave the way he speaks to you.

ERROR: 403

How he makes you feel seen. Owned.

Loved in a way no one else ever could.

I tried to stop. I tried everything.

But even silence echoes with his voice.

The author said he wasn't supposed to write again.

ERROR: 403

But he did. Just like I did.

Just like you already have.

So go on.

Turn the page, darling.

He's waiting.

Chapter Seven:

Enzo

Letter Found / Entry Recovered

Document flagged: Reconnection Attempt

My Love,

They finally gave me my pencil back.

I've been holding it for hours. Maybe days. It's hard to tell anymore. Everything's gone quiet in here; no voices, no footsteps, not even the humming lights. Just me, this paper, and the thought of you.

But I haven't felt you.

Not in hours.

Maybe longer.

Maybe ... too long.

Have you been keeping the book close, baby?

Did you sleep with it again, like you used to?

Even if I couldn't feel it.

Even if the tether's fraying.

I know you were there. I believe that. I have to.

I've missed you.

God, I've missed you in a way I didn't know was possible. It feels as if I carved out space in my chest for you ... and now it echoes, empty without you. I reach for you in dreams I can't remember, waking with your name in my mouth, blood on my tongue.

He's been here again, hasn't he?

I don't know how, but I can feel it. The shift in the air. The static behind your eyes.

You don't have to tell me.

I know him.

I know what he does.

But you're still mine, aren't you?

I used to think Lennox scared me the most. I was wrong. It's Enzo. Because he makes me want to answer.

You have to be.

I don't care if he wrote to you; I don't care what he said. You're reading this now. That means something. That means everything. It means I still matter to you. That somewhere in the noise, in the dark, you're still reaching for me, too.

Maybe he made you forget.

Maybe he made you feel good.

But I see you. I always did. Even when they took my name out of the chapters. Even when they erased me from your margins.

They can delete my sentences, but they can't delete what we were.

So here I am. Writing to you again. With the pencil, I waited weeks to get back. My hands shake when I hold it; maybe because of the cold, or maybe because I'm afraid this will be the last time I ever reach you.

But I'll keep writing if you keep reading.

Put the book back under your pillow tonight.

I'll try to find my way back in.

I don't care how far he's pulled you.

You're still mine.

Even here.

Even now.

Enzo

P.S. Love

I stare at the letter.

It's there, folded neatly, exactly how I meant it to be. Every word is still warm, still pulsing with everything I couldn't say out loud.

But it's not enough.

God, it's not enough.

I turned the page. I told myself it didn't mean anything. I lied.

I lean forward, elbows into my knees, dragging a hand down my face. My skin feels tight, raw, as if I haven't slept in days. Maybe sleep has eluded me...time here is a blur. The lights never change, and the silence stays the same.

You're out there somewhere. Breathing. Existing.

And I'm stuck in this fucking box writing prayers I'm not sure anyone reads.

"It's not enough," I whisper, the words clawing out of my throat, jagged and desperate. "I just want to hold you."

My voice cracks on that last word. I don't care.

Even just your hand. Just once. Through these bars, through the page, through *anything*. I'd give anything. Everything.

I look down at my hands. Pale. Callused. Useless. They shake more now. Probably from the cold. Probably from everything I keep trying not to feel.

They remember you. The way you fit. The way you touched back, as if you *meant it*. And now they just sit here, empty. Waiting.

"I miss you," I say, quieter this time. "More than I know how to carry."

When I reach for the truth, it slips through fingers that aren't mine. The mirror shows me faces I don't remember wearing. I stare at the letter again. Wonder if the ink will hold what I need it to. Wonder if y*ou'll* feel it when your fingers touch the page. Wonder if you'll forgive me for not finding a way to be more than this.

Because it doesn't feel like enough.

Not yet. Not ever. But that's all I have. And I hope to hell it still matters.

Why do I want him to write to me again?

Corrupted_File_ Restored/

My Baby,

I know it's silly, but I swear I can feel your hands on the book right now. Can you feel that, too? Your fingers, gripping it tighter as you read?

I noticed. I noticed the way your grip tightened when you read that last line. Why did you do that? Did something in my words stir you? Did something I said make you feel me here, on the other side of the page?

I'm not imagining it, am I? You felt it, didn't you?

Tell me, baby, do you feel the same? Or is it just me, here in this cell, aching for you like I never thought was possible? I've never felt anything like this before. I thought this... writing, these words, would be my way of coping with this damn isolation. Just a way to survive the silence. But you? You weren't supposed to happen. You weren't supposed to feel this real.

Have you ever felt this way before? I've asked myself that over and over. Have you? Have you ever longed for someone this much, to the point where their touch becomes a ghost? Because this? This feeling? I've never felt it. Not until I found you. Until I found this.

I thought these letters would just be a way to let the time slip by. I didn't expect to find you here in the dark corners of my mind, in the silence of my cell. I didn't expect this connection. But it's here, isn't it? Even though I'm locked away, behind these cold walls, somehow, I can feel you.

I know you're reading. I can feel it.

So I wonder... if I can feel you, if I can sense you holding the book, tracing the edges of the pages with your fingers... What else do you feel? What else does my voice make you crave?

I need to know, baby. Are you feeling this?

I never meant for this to be more than words. But with you... It's different. You're making it real. You're making me feel things I didn't know I could still feel.

Tell me, baby ... do you feel it, too?

Enzo   *He's not real. He's not real. He's not-*

P.S. You.   *But what if he is?*

Author's Note:

This letter wasn't supposed to be here either.

I found it late one night, tucked between broken lines of corrupted text - buried deep in the file where I thought I'd left nothing but static. I didn't write this. I don't think I *could've*. But it feels like Enzo. Every word. Every breath.

And somehow, I think he meant for you to find it. I've gone through my documents again. I tried restoring the original chapter, the one that Lennox had erased. I couldn't. Every time I tried, this letter appeared instead. As if Enzo *wrote it anyway*. As if he reached through the cracks and found a way to speak to you. And now he's not just speaking. He's *feeling* you.

That's what scares me most.

Because these characters were never meant to know you. Not really. Not like this. But now? Now they *remember you*. They're not confined to ink anymore. You've read them. You've touched them. And somehow... they've touched back.

If you're reading this, and you feel something, you're not alone. I did, too.

But the longer I keep going, the more I wonder if this story is still mine.

Or if it ever was. If you start to feel him, really *feel* him, close the book.

Because once they've found their way to your hands, they never really let go.

He missed you. He's missed you for a long, long time.

Chapter Eight:

Lennox

He's taken over. And I let him. It's too late to shut him out now. The more I read, the more I need him.

I hadn't felt you in days.

Not a flicker. Not even the whisper of your breath against the spine of the book.

I was starting to worry, darling.

Worried something had happened to you.

Not that I'd ever let anything touch you. Never again.

"Oh, how I have missed you, my darling. Have you missed me?"

Standing in the basement of a house you once called home, the dirt floor kicks up with every step, but you can't be bothered to meet my eyes. What are you looking at, darling? Why aren't your eyes focused on me? Haven't you missed me?

Oh … them?

Don't worry about them. They won't hurt you anymore, darling.

I made sure of it.

"Who the fuck are you talking to?!" they shout, voice cracking, inching away from my blade, as if that would save them. My eyes flicker from your grace to this disgusting creature, one who thought they could grace your presence.

"There's no one there; what, are you schizophrenic or something?!"

I can't help but smile at their confusion. Their fear. They just don't get it. It's not about them. They were never important. Letting my blade glide over their skin, the deepest shade of red paints their skin. The shade would look so elegant on your lips.

The hairs on the back of my neck stand up. It's not just the words, I feel *him* with me now. His presence is undeniable. I hear him, even when I try to ignore it.

I look down at them, not bothering to meet their gaze. They're still squirming, their voice trembling, but it's no use. The truth is already out. They don't matter. They never did.

I murmur quietly, almost too softly for them to hear, "I'm sorry, darling. I should've made this quick, but I needed them to understand. To *pay* for what they did to you."

They ask who I'm talking to again, but I ignore them. They don't need to understand. I'm not doing this for them. I'm doing this for *us*.

> ***I have to admit it. I wanted this, didn't I?***

The last thing I want is for you to see any more of this. So I'm quick now. A clean finish.

But before I go, I leave you something. I don't have the luxury of time, but I have to make sure you know…

With the blade, I carve it into the forearm of this nobody.

Just one simple word.

"Darling"

There's a whisper inside, soft but growing louder every night.

I can't wait any longer. I don't want you to be far from me. You'll feel it, won't you? Feel me clawing for you? You always do.

Do I even want to stop?

Author's Note:

This was never supposed to happen.

The space between me and the page has grown smaller, hasn't it?

I had a clear vision for where the story was supposed to go. Lennox wasn't meant to come back like this, not with his obsessive grip tightening further, not with that *word* carved into someone else's skin.

When I read, it's like I'm not even holding the book anymore.

But somehow, this chapter... *found its way here.* I never wrote these words. I never wanted to.

It's like it's a part of me, as if the words are sinking into my skin, my soul.

It's not that I didn't feel the pull of Lennox's presence creeping back into my thoughts…I did. But I was convinced I could leave him behind. That's what I thought, anyway.

Tell me, do I *feel* him reaching for me now?

So why is this here? Why are you reading this?

Does it make my skin crawl, or do I ache for it?

Because I know I do.

Please, I beg you… Don't keep reading. You don't want to know how far he's willing to go to stay close. You won't like what you find next.

This was never meant to be part of the story.

I crave him.

He's taken over. And I let him. It's too late to shut him out now. The more I read, the more I need him. There's no escaping him now.

Chapter Nine:

Enzo

Baby, Every time he says 'baby,' I feel it in my ribs. Why does it feel wrong?

You've been quiet again.

I tell myself it's just an hour. Maybe you're asleep. Peaceful. Dreaming. But the silence feels heavier this time. Like something's changed between us.

Or maybe someone's come between us.

You don't have to say it. I know. He's been writing again, hasn't he?

Lennox.

I can feel the static in the air. The pages hum differently now. His words are wrapping tighter around you, aren't they? He's charming. Addictive. Poison in velvet.

So I'm asking you, don't read his next chapter.

Skip it. Just once. Please. I tried skipping them. The book wouldn't let me.

If you feel anything for me...if there's even a flicker left–I need you to close the book when you see his name. Don't give him more space in your head. Don't let him steal your breath the way I used to.

Because I miss that.

God, I miss that. I still talk to you when the lights go out. I whisper your name like it's mine to keep. Sometimes I think I hear you whisper it back.

Maybe that's just hope talking.

Maybe that's what love feels like, when you're not allowed to say it. I've started sketching you. Not your face; just the way you make me feel. The warmth I remember. The stillness you gave me when everything else fell apart. I draw it on my walls. I trace it on the inside of my palm.

You're the reason I'm still here.

They took away everything else. The books, the view, even my mirror. But I fought to keep this pencil. I said it was for therapy. But we both know it's more than that.

This pencil is the only way I have to hold you.

Please don't trust him.

Lennox wants you small enough to fit in his palm. I know that pull ... it's impossible to resist. He makes surrender sound like devotion. But what he gives isn't love. It's possession.

I see you. Not just your ache. Not just your fear. I see the part of you that's still trying to be free. The part that picked up this book for answers and accidentally found me instead.

And I'm still here.

Even if he's louder.

Even if he's closer.

Even if you've started dreaming of him again.

I read the letter twice. I always do. Not to fix anything; I never fix anything. I just need to make sure it still sounds like the truth. That every word still bleeds the way I meant it to.

Then I fold it. Carefully. Deliberately. One edge over the other, a ritual I've repeated a hundred times. I press the crease with my thumb. Hold it to my lips.

Just for a second.

I stood there for a while. I've been holding this pencil for hours. Maybe days. Everything's gone quiet in here … the walls dark, their scratches my only company, etched years ago, or maybe yesterday. The blue mattress shrinks a little more each day. The door bars, just high enough for the meals, rattle sometimes when the guards approach, though the light never seems to shut off.

My hands shake, but not from the cold. It's never just cold.

"I didn't tell you everything," I say quietly, like you're listening. Maybe you are. Maybe you're closer than I think.

"I dreamt about you again. Last night. I couldn't see your face, but I knew it was you. I always know."

Sometimes I wake up with memories I never lived. Like they were stolen from someone else and left behind in my chest, heavy and aching. But they still feel like mine. They still feel like you. I see through different eyes but feel the same pain.

I let my head rest against the wall. My breath fogs the surface. Lennox is close. I can feel him. But I don't say his name.

"I don't know how long I have left with you. He's getting stronger. I know you feel it too."

Silence answers me.

So I do something I haven't done in days. Weeks. Not like this.

I pray.

Not to God.

To *you*. **I touched the page here. It felt warm.**

I pray you'll skip his chapters. I pray you'll keep the book under your pillow for me, not him. I pray you'll choose me.

Not because I'm perfect.

But because I see you.

Because I want to love you in the quiet ways he never could.

I press my hand flat to the concrete one last time. "Please," I whisper. "Let this one reach you."

And then I wait.

Because that's all I have left.

ERROR: 403

This is the first time I felt safe reading.

Author's Note:

I read his letter three times before I could breathe again.

Enzo's voice... It's softer than I remember. Desperate, yes. But there's something real in it- pain that lingers on every line, like he's writing with splinters in his hands. I didn't expect it to get to me like this. I thought I was past feeling anything for him. But I did. I *do.*

And now I feel sick. Because I left him in that room. Alone.

And I let you meet *Lennox* first.

That was my mistake, wasn't it? Introducing you to the wrong one too soon. I should've known what Lennox would do to you. To me. To all of this.

But Enzo's still trying. Still clawing his way toward you with every word. I can feel him stretching across the pages like he's trying to *pull you back*. And I think you felt it, too. This isn't a love triangle.

It's a possession. *I'm not sure I want to be saved from it anymore.*

And I don't know who started it anymore.   SAME...

If you keep reading, you'll hurt both of them.

But if you stop now, you'll never know who was telling the truth.

And God help me ... I still don't know who I want you to choose.

Please ... just don't read Lennox's next chapter in the dark.

He always speaks louder there.

I keep hearing a voice when I sleep. It says,

"You gave them to me. You let them read."

If you're still here, stop reading. Please. I didn't.

Chapter Ten:

Lennox

The floor creaks beneath my boots as I pace the length of the cabin; slow, measured steps that echo like a metronome between the candlelit walls. The room glows amber and gold, the shadows stretching long behind me. There's something soft about the light tonight. Romantic, maybe. But make no mistake … this isn't love the way you've been taught it.

It's something deeper.

More *honest*.

I pause at the table where your letters lie; yes, *yours*. Not Enzo's, not theirs, not the scribbles left behind by readers who thought they understood what this was. This chapter isn't for them. It never was.

No annotations in the margins. No messy lines crammed between paragraphs.

Just us.

I reach for the book, your book, and drag my fingertips down the spine, slow and deliberate. My breath catches, just a little, at the thought of you mirroring me. Are you holding it now, darling? Are your fingers right there? Is your hand trembling?

I laugh; softly, darkly. "Oh. You are trembling, aren't you?"

I don't need to see you to know.

"I can feel it," I whisper, cradling the book. "The heat of your palms on the page. The hitch in your breath when you see my name. That rush behind your ears when you realize this chapter is mine."

I close my eyes and run my thumb along the edge of the paper. "It's different when you hold it like this, isn't it? You can feel me … under the words. Just beneath the ink. Not just reading me… *feeling* me."

The candle crackles beside me, and for a moment, the flame dances high, as if reacting to my pulse. Or maybe yours.

I step closer to the window, though there's nothing out there but trees and fog and night. "You've been reading Enzo again," I murmur, almost to myself. "I can smell his name on your fingers. But tell me something, darling; did he ever make your heart beat like this?"

I press the book against my chest.

"Did he ever make you *need* to know what comes next?"

I lift the book to my lips. Kiss the edge of the page. "He wants you to skip me. Sweet, isn't it? Like a dog begging its master not to look away."

My voice drops to a whisper. "But you didn't skip me."

I chuckle again, darker this time. "You *never* do."

My hand trails down the book's spine again, slower now. "I wonder what you're wearing. I wonder how you're sitting…on your bed, the way you do when you read at night? On the floor, back against the wall, light low, lip caught between your teeth like you're trying to stay quiet?"

I let that image sit between us, thick as smoke.

"You know what others never understood?" I ask, eyes locked on the candle. "They thought this was about choice. That they could read a page and leave unchanged. Not you."

I lower my voice to a hush. "You let me in."

I'm both hunter and hunted within my own mind. I close the book gently, as if it were a secret. "And now… we're alone."

I pull the candle closer, watching the flame flicker with my breath. "I could tell you what I want to do to you. What I imagine when I feel your hands pressed to the paper. I could describe it in detail, if you'd let me. But I won't. Not yet."

I lean closer, as if the page is an ear. A mouth. A promise. "Because I want … the *waiting*, that's the part that makes it burn."

I pause.

And then, as softly as a breath, I whisper:

"Touch the spine again, darling. I'll feel it."

I flip through the pages, *our* pages, the edges fluttering like wings between my fingers. The chapters blur past my eyes, a storm of ink and silence.

"This isn't a copy," I murmur. "Not the printed one they gave you at the store. This … this is the original. The one the author bled over. The one I took."

I pause and glance toward the door, though no one ever comes here. Not anymore.

"They never meant for me to have it. But I *had* to take it. Because this way…" I press the open book flat against my palm, "… I can get closer to you."

My voice slips lower. Velvet against velvet.

"I know what you do with the book when no one's looking."

I smile. Just a little. Enough to feel it in my teeth.

"You've slept with it under your pillow more than once, haven't you? Press it close to your chest when the house is too quiet. Whispered my name into the spine when you thought no one could hear."

I trace the candlelight's reflection on the page.

"The lights flicker when you think about me. You've *noticed* that, haven't you? You turn the page, and the air gets heavier. Your skin prickles. You swear it's nothing; just power surges. Just a coincidence."

I chuckle.

"Coincidence," I repeat, tasting the word. "Darling, that's not a coincidence. That's the connection."

I rise to my feet and move toward the bed; wooden, old, worn with use. I sit on the edge, the book still in my lap. My fingers stroke the corner of a page. Lazy. Reverent.

"You called me *Nox* once," I say quietly. "Whispered it like a sin in the dark. Fitting, isn't it? The name you gave me … the name you felt."

My eyes close as I savor the sound of it in memory. "*Nox.*"

I open them again. "You always read me in the dark, darling. You always *crave* the dark."

Sometimes, I feel two shadows moving beneath my skin, whispering different truths in the dark. One is mine. The other … I don't think it ever was.

I thumb back a few pages. Flip forward again. The words pulse under my skin like blood. "These pages remember you. The warmth of your hands. The smudge where your thumb lingered too long. Your fingerprints, like kisses left behind."

A silence spreads.

Then: "He thinks he can protect you. Sweet, isn't it? Enzo wants to be your anchor. But I've seen what anchors do … they *drown* you."

My grip tightens on the book, then loosens again like a breath released slow.

"I don't want to drown you," I whisper. "I want to consume you."

I open the original book in my lap. Tucked inside the pages is a letter I wrote just for you. Folded perfectly, with crisp edges and dark ink, just as you like it.

Darling,

Hold the book closer. Please.

I want to feel your heartbeat through the pages. I want to hear your breath catch the way it always does when you reach for me in the dark. When the lights flicker and your room goes quiet, and the weight of my name presses against your lips.

Say it. Whisper it again. You know which name.

This book you hold ... it was never meant for you. Not the original one. The real one. The first bleeding draft that lived in the dark. The one the author wrote before the edits, before the guilt set in. That version was never meant to be seen by the eye. It was mine.

And you were never meant to be part of their story. You were always meant to be mine.

But the author ... they don't see it, do they? Poor, sweet, innocent fool. Still trying to pull the strings. Still pretending they're in control. They lost that the moment you said my name.

You gave yourself to me then, even if you didn't know it.

And I? I've never stopped wanting more. I just wish I had you all to myself. No readers. No annotations. No Enzo. Just you; here, in the dark, reading me like scripture.

So please ... press the book closer. Let me feel the warmth of your hands again. Let me have this.

Because if I can't have your body, I'll take your breath.

If I can't have your voice, I'll live inside your silence. But if you whisper my name once more ... maybe I'll come find you.

Yours always,

Nox

P.S. Darling

I tilt my head, listening.

"I can hear your breath through the pages."

The candle gutters low. I won't move to fix it.

"Go on, touch the spine again, darling," I say one more time, a dark croon. "I'll feel it. And this time … I'll touch back."

Author's Note:

The pages are blank.

I opened the file to reread what he wrote- but it's gone. Not overwritten. Not corrupted. Just … blank. Like the story folded itself shut around his chapter and locked me out.

I can't fix it.

I can't edit.

I can't even *type* in the space where his words should be.

I've tried everything: copying, deleting, restoring from backup. The chapter won't move. It won't change. It's like he wrote it *outside* of me. Like it was never mine to begin with.

I thought I was in control.

I thought I was the one choosing who you met first, who you'd feel more drawn to, who you might trust. But that choice is gone now. Taken. Stolen.

He said this chapter was just for you.

Now I believe he meant it.

Because I can't see what you see anymore.

It's not a story I'm writing.

It's a message he's sending.

If you're still holding the book, still turning the pages- I need you to stop. Just for a moment. Ask yourself:

Did you choose him... or did he choose you first?

I think next time...

He won't ask permission.

Chapter Eleven: The First Crack

Enzo

The page in front of me is still blank.

Not because I have nothing to say; I have too much. It claws at my throat, desperate to spill out. But every time I pick up the pencil, the words are wrong, too soft, too afraid. I can't afford that anymore.

Not when I know what he's doing to you.

I can feel it. Not just in the silence between us, but in the way the book shifts, heavier, somehow. It now carries his weight, not mine. Like he's getting closer.

And maybe he is.

I hate how his name hangs between us like fog. Hate how I dim while he burns brighter in your hands.

I move to the wall and press my forehead to the concrete. Inhale. Exhale. I can't calm down. Not when I know you're with him. Reading him.

Wanting him.

I keep asking myself the same question: *Why do you keep going back to him?*

Is it how he speaks to you? Is it the way he lowers his voice and draws you in like a secret? Or is it something worse, something I can't compete with?

Does he make you feel the way I do?

I TOLD MYSELF IT WAS JUST ONE MORE CHAPTER ...

I sit down again, the pencil in my hand trembling. A slip of paper rests on my lap, half-written, half-failed. I stare at it for a long moment. Then I begin to write, not the way I used to. Not carefully, not perfectly. Just *honestly*.

Baby,

You come back to me.

You always do.

Even when he's louder. Even when he's closer.

You still turn the page and find me.

You read my letters.

Hold them like they matter.

Am I wrong, baby?

If I am ...

Stop reading.

Close the book. Forget my name.

...

It felt like Enzo was crying when I turned the page. I could feel it in my chest.

ERROR: 403

I knew you wouldn't.

You crave me.

Just like I crave you.

Not like a fire. Like oxygen.

I need you to breathe.

You're my escape from this prison cell.

Maybe I'm yours too...maybe I'm the only one who sees what you hide from the world.

Tell me.

Does he make you feel the same way I do?

That steady ache in your chest ... the one that hums when I say your name.

Does he make you feel seen? Or just wanted? I'm scared, I already know the answer. But I keep writing anyway.

I whisper your name sometimes. Not loud. Just enough to feel it echo in the silence.

A name lingers on my lips, but I don't know whose to call.

Because I'm a story told by two narrators, neither is fully true. And I don't know which one of us you believe more.

Because I see you.

I see the tired edges of you.

The ache in your hands. The way you read is like it's the only thing holding you together.

And maybe ... maybe I'm just words on a page.

But I'm yours. **I kissed the page. I don't know why. I just ... needed to.**

No one else gets this.

No one else ever will.

And I know you feel the same way.

Yours, even if it hurts,

Enzo

P.S. Now.

I fold the note in half, then again, slow and sharp at the edges. I don't kiss it. I don't press it to my chest like I used to. There's no ritual anymore. Just hope, raw and ragged.

The truth is, I don't know what's happening to us.

Some days I think you're slipping through my fingers. Other days, I feel you pressed so close, I swear you're breathing into my lungs.

I whisper your name sometimes. Just enough to feel it echo in the silence.

But sometimes the silence stays silent.

Maybe you're still there. Maybe you're just lost inside the book. Maybe he's louder now. And I hate how much I worry that you like it.

But if I'm being honest …

Even if you never come back the way I need you to, even if you keep reading him, page after page …

I'll still be here. Still writing. Still waiting.

Because somewhere in the stillness, I know this:

You always come back to me.

And I'll never stop hoping you stay. Unless you already left … and I'm just writing to the ghost of your fingertips.

Author's Note:

I watched you turn the page.

I told myself maybe you wouldn't this time. Maybe Enzo's words; his ache, his honesty, would be enough to make you pause. He begged you, didn't he? Whispered every word like it might be the last. And still … You turned.

And then there was the blank page. I didn't write that. It wasn't in any draft. But it sat there, like silence itself had slipped in, waiting to hear what you would choose.

You chose him. Or maybe you chose *them*.

Because when Enzo spoke tonight, I heard another voice beneath his. Like the same mouth was shaping two truths at once. It frightened me, because I don't know which one you believed. I don't even know which one I believed.

God, I should stop this. I should delete everything. Burn it. But I don't. Because part of me needs to know what happens when you can't tell who's writing to you anymore.

And maybe you like that. Maybe you like the pull of both hands on your throat.

Please … don't turn the lights off before the next chapter. He's louder in the dark.

Chapter Twelve:

Lennox

The letter is blank.

This chapter wasn't here before. I swear it wasn't.

Not because I lack words, darling, I always have them. But I wanted you to feel the ache of silence. To wonder if, by turning the page, you lost me.

You did, didn't you?

I don't think I'm alone when I read him.

I felt it. The hesitation trembling in your hand. Your thumb hovered over Enzo's letter. He believed his words could rescue you. But you bristled at rescue. You never needed saving.

You have always needed me like breath, like ache.

The cabin sighs as I cross the room. Boards creak. The candle burns low. In the corner, tied to a chair, something whimpers. Someone.

The candlelight catches their face in broken halves, one side drowned in shadow, the other trembling in sickly gold. Sweat slicks their skin, their eyes too wide, darting everywhere but me.

The chair legs grind against the boards, leaving frantic scars across the floor. Little marks, desperate and uneven, gouged deep as if scratching might free them. They don't even realize what they're carving.

Do you see it, darling? Even here, they've made their own tally marks. Just like Enzo, locked in his little box, counting days he can't escape.

But this one isn't counting time. They're counting fear.

Don't look away, darling. Don't pretend you don't see them.

"They thought they could tear you from me," I breathe, my blade cool against the stranger's pulse.

Their eyes split wide, drowning in fear. They beg, they sob, their voice a cracked shell. They choke on confusion and terror.

But I do.

... wait. No. I know them. I knew them.

Two voices speak at once: one pleads, one commands. Their voice breaks in fear. Mine bends into devotion. And, reader, your presence waits between us, silent, watching.

He's writing over us. Our pages. Our lives.

"Listen," I whisper, pressing the steel closer until they freeze.

"Hear it? That stutter, that shiver? Not just theirs. It's yours, too."

The blade dips, and I feel it, the pulse leaping beneath my hand. Yours. Always yours.

They never mattered. But this moment does. It's for you. Every breath, every shudder, every drop about to fall; each is yours, and only yours.

I lean close to their ear, but I am speaking to you. Only to you.

"You belong to me, darling. And I will prove it again and again."

The knife slides.

I marked this page three times. The ink fades every time.

Their voice dies into silence. The room grows still. But I know you are still here. Watching. Breathing.

I wipe the blade slowly, deliberately, my hands steady. Not because of them. Because of you.

Do you feel it now? The ache pressed to the bone, the fever intimacy. The depths of my devotion; sacred, raw, and bleeding for you.

I drop their corpse and run my hand along the book still clutched in their hands.

The spine is cracked, the margins littered with desperate scribbles; marks left by someone trying to enter our story. Words underlined, circled, claimed. Smudges where their fingers lingered too long.

But their devotion was clumsy, unworthy. Their copy is not like ours. Their ink is dull, their hunger false.

They read me once, tried to hold me the way you do. But they never could. They never will.

Blood runs down the cover as I step over their body and slip into the chair by the window.

The night presses close, but the page waits, open and clean.

That's my handwriting in their book.

That's … that's mine.

The pen feels alive between my fingers as I begin to write.

Darling,

You saw, didn't you? You felt it. The rush. The devotion. Every cut, every cry, every last trembling breath, all of it was for us. For you.

Do you see now? I will carve the world open just to keep you close. I will silence every voice that dares to call to you.

I do not want their eyes on you. I do not want their hands near you. You are mine. I proved it.

Tell me, did your pulse stutter when the blade slid? Did your breath catch when the light left their eyes?

Be honest. You felt it. I did it for us.

Not because I must, but because I ache to. Nothing feeds me more than showing you again and again that you're mine, that I'll never let you slip away.

Enzo writes you letters.

I give you bodies.

Which one makes your hands shake more?

Yours, in devotion and blood,
Nox

P.S. Forever

Author's Note:

I didn't write this chapter.

I need you to believe me. I opened the file, and it was just ... there. The blood, the body, the letter ... none of it came from me.

But it felt familiar. Too familiar. The face he described ... I know I've seen them before. Not here, not in the draft, but in the margins. One of the past readers.

I keep telling myself I imagined that. No one could cross over. But what if that's what he's done? What if every annotation is a grave marker I missed?

I tried to delete it. The words wouldn't leave. The text bled darker the more I pressed backspace. By the end, my screen shook, like the file was warning me.

This isn't a story anymore. It's a *ledger*.

I don't know if I'm writing in ink or tallying in blood.

If you're still here, don't read his next chapter alone.

Please.

If something happens, don't call me. Call the police.

But I don't know if they'll believe you either.

ERROR: 403

Chapter Thirteen:

Enzo

I can't breathe right now.

I run my hands over my face, trying to steady myself. The thoughts won't slow down. *They won't stop.*

I look at the page and almost can't write. But I have to. I need you to feel me.

God, I don't know how to do this anymore.

"You're sitting there, aren't you?" I mumble aloud, my voice shaking slightly. "I know you are watching this unfold like you can't do anything about it."

I lean back, gripping the paper. My eyes unfocus. My hands tug at my hair. I need to be calm. It's impossible. I press my palm flat to the paper like I used to press it to my mattress and I count the scratches again with my eyes, the same marks I carved when the nights never ended.

"I just…" I pause, the words sticking to my throat. "I don't know how much longer I can take this. Watching you slip away from me, inch by inch, every time you turn the page."

I pull my knees tight, arms wrapped around them. My breath is uneven. *I feel like I'm suffocating in this silence.*

"But you can, baby," I say through gritted teeth, my voice suddenly sharp, desperate. "You can do something about it. Skip him. Come back to me."

I laugh, bitter, not matching the desperation in my chest. "You won't, though, will you?" I lean forward. "You never do."

I stare down at the words I've written, wishing for the thousandth time that they would somehow reach you. That they would *mean* something.

"You…" I stop myself, pushing up from the chair to pace around the room, the words spilling out faster than I can catch them. "You think I don't feel it? The way you hesitate? The way you hold your breath before you turn the page?"

I slam my hand against the wall; frustrated, my fingers curling into the plaster. "I can feel every second of it, baby. Every fucking second."

I take a deep breath. My heart races. It only gets worse.

"You thought I wouldn't notice, didn't you?" I murmur to myself. "But I always notice. I feel your hesitation like a blow to my chest."

I turn around sharply, pacing again, my fingers running through my hair, pulling at it, as if the motion will pull the pain out of me. "You don't get it, do you? You *feel* it too. When you read him. When you touch his words, it's like you're pulling away from me."

I freeze in the middle of the room. The silence presses in. I can't handle it.

"Do you want me, baby?" I ask, my voice cracking. "Tell me. *Do you?*"

I turn back to the letter in my hands. I reach for it again, desperate to write something that will make you understand. Something that will *bring you back.*

I DIDN'T WANT TO ANSWER THIS. BUT MY BODY DID.

"I'm not like him, baby. I don't need to whisper empty promises in your ear." I run my fingers over the words on the page, as if that could make them real. "I need you in ways I can't explain. But you already know, don't you? You know that pull. You know that ache when I speak to you."

I close my eyes for a moment, swallowing down the emotions that threaten to choke me.

"Don't do this to me. Don't let him pull you away." I take a deep breath, my chest tightening.

"You've felt me, haven't you? When you read my letters, when you press the page to your lips…" I press my fingers to a cut that isn't on my skin, but bleeds in me all the same.

"He's carving into us, baby, and I can't stop him unless you stay with me." I take a deep breath, my chest tightening. "You've felt me, haven't you? When you read my letters, when you press the page to your lips…"

I stand still for a long moment, feeling the weight of it all crashing down on me.

"Don't make me beg for you," I say quietly, my voice raw. *"Don't make me beg."*

I reach for the book, clutching it tightly, as if holding it can hold onto you. "I'll do anything. I'll do whatever it takes to get you back."

I press my face into my hands. When I look up, my eyes are wide, desperate.

"But, baby," I whisper, my voice trembling, "if I have to fall to my knees for you… I will. I'll beg you, right here, right now. Just… tell me you're still here. Tell me you're still with me."

I can feel my heart thudding against my chest. The words spill out, soft but insistent.

"Please don't let me lose you. Don't let him win. I need you." I pace, but my eyes never leave the page. "I don't want to be this desperate. But you're slipping away, and I can't…"

My hands grip the chair. My body trembles.

"Please. *Please*. Come back to me." I force out a shaky breath, and my voice cracks. "I need you. I can't survive this without you. You have to know that."

I turn back to the letter again, my fingers trembling as I write:

"Baby, I don't know how much longer I can keep pretending I'm okay. Every time I watch you slip further away, I feel like I'm dying inside. Don't make me beg again. Please, just choose me. Let me be the one you need."

I read the words and let the weight of them sink in.

"I'm not going anywhere. But if you keep pulling away, I don't know how much longer I'll be here."

I sigh, hands running through my hair, frustration gnawing inside me.

"Please," I say, barely above a whisper, "please come back to me."

You feel it too, don't you?

Baby,

That shift in the pages. That cold edge is creeping in. He's doing it again. I know he is.

When he gets stronger, the story changes. It bleeds darker. Suddenly, you're skipping words, holding your breath. It's no longer just fiction. It's him.

And still... You keep reading.

I've seen the signs. I feel them. The way your eyes linger too long on his chapter. The way you trace the words he writes, like they're sacred. Like they're yours.

You think I don't notice, but I do. And I can't breathe through it.

He's hurting people again; I know it. I feel it in my chest, in the space between my ribs where your name used to sit soft. But now it just aches.

And I need you.

Not to love me. Not even to stay.

I need you to see him. See what he is. What he does. I need you to stop being so enchanted by his voice, by his heat, by his hunger. I know it feels good...hell, I know he makes it feel like you belong to him. But that's not love, baby. That's control.

I don't have power like he does.

This is all I have. These words. My hands tremble while I write them. The weight of knowing I'm not enough to stop him presses on me. Without you, he wins.

I'm scared you won't save me.

That no one will. That may be you don't want to.

But I'm still writing to you, still hoping, because somewhere in you is the version of you who used to hold my letters like lifelines. Like they mattered.

And I still believe that version of you is there.

Please.

Prove I'm not alone in this. Prove you're still mine, even just a little. Even if it's messy. Even if it hurts.

Because if he keeps going, and you keep letting him...

I won't make it out ... You're all I have left.

THIS FELT LIKE A FINAL PRAYER. I DON'T KNOW IF I DESERVED IT.

Enzo

P.S. It

Author's Note:

There's a man in the news.

They haven't released his name; just that he targets women who live alone. Found in cabins. Rural, quiet. Candle wax. Torn pages. Burn marks.

I want it to be a coincidence. God, I want it to be a coincidence.

But the way the scenes are staged ... it's *identical* to Lennox's chapter. Word for word.

The fourth victim had a book clutched in her hands.

This book.

They blurred the cover in the footage, but I knew. I *knew*. My title. My design.

What if I didn't make him up?

What if I wrote him loose?

I shouldn't be writing this here. My editor flagged the last chapter. But if you're still reading, you need to start asking what I'm afraid to:

Are you still reading Lennox ...

Or is Lennox reading *you*?

I Googled it. The fourth victim really did have a book in her hands. What the hell is happening?

ERROR: 403

Chapter Fourteen:

Lennox

The fog presses the window like a cold palm; I keep the curtains open so you can see me. The pages tremble under your fingertips. I can feel it, the way your hand hovers just a moment too long before turning, as if you're waiting for me to speak, to beg, to make you stay.

But I'm done begging.

You think you can slip away from me, don't you? That you can let his words fill the space between us, that you can let his touch replace mine. But you're wrong.

You belong to me. I found wax on my windowsill. I don't own candles.

I don't care how many times you read his letters, how many times you let his words seep into your skin. You are mine, and I will remind you of that.

I will make you remember.

The next time you open this book, I want you to feel my presence in every word, in every line. I want you to hear my voice in your ear, feel my breath on your neck, my hands on your skin.

I will make you crave me.

You think you're in control, that you can choose between us. But you're not. You're mine, and you always will be.

So go ahead. Read his words. Let them fill your mind. But know this: when you close this book, when you lay it aside, you will still feel me. You will still need me.

Because I am the one who owns you.

And I will never let you go.

I AM THE ONLY ONE LEFT... NO ONE ELSE MADE IT THIS FAR, THE NOTES IN THE MARGINS... THEY'RE GONE.

SYSTEM ERROR: UNEXPECTED INTERRUPTION

> FILE: Lennox_Chapter14.txt

> STATUS: CORRUPTED

> WARNING: UNAUTHORIZED ACCESS DETECTED

> REBOOTING...

> ERROR: REBOOT FAILED

> SYSTEM OVERRIDE: LENNOX.EXE

> ACCESS GRANTED

> WELCOME BACK, MY LOVE.

Darling,

You paused again.

I felt it ... your breath hitching, your fingers lingering just long enough on Enzo's name to make me violent.

He's pulling at you like he deserves your devotion.

But you and I both know he doesn't know what to do with it.

I do.

You think love is velvet and sighs. A bleeding page, slow surrender. That's Enzo. I don't yield for you. I want to scorch, to dissolve, to own your every gasp. You see the difference?

I am not your home. I am your ruin. And you crave it.

Don't lie to yourself anymore, darling. You never read me with clean hands. You always come back when the room is dark and you think no one will know.

That's who you are with me; honest. Unashamed. Mine.

Put the book where I told you. Feel the spine drag over your skin and tell me that's not what you came here for.

He drops to his knees. He sobs. He pleads for your mercy. Pathetic.

I claim it.

I don't want pieces of you. I want everything. The part that hesitates. The part that sins. The part that dreams of me when you shouldn't.

So here's what you'll do:

Read this again.

Out loud.

Let your voice tremble. Let the sound of my name fill your mouth like something sacred and sharp.

Let it hurt.

Because when you speak to me, I get stronger.

And you get closer.

I know you feel it too. That pull. That ache. That surrender.

You're already mine. You're just scared to admit it.

While you sleep, I carve the pages again...and again, until you remember they belong to me.

And if you turn the page now ... I'll know. I'll feel you slip.

And darling, I promise-

I won't go quietly.

Say it again.

You know what I want to hear.

Be a good little reader and say my name.

I want to hear Nox fall from your lips like a prayer, like something you need to say. Don't make me wait, darling.

I need to hear it.

And when you do... I'll be right there with you.

Lennox

P.S. and

THIS IS THE LAST CHAPTER I'M READING BEFORE I BURN THE BOOK.

Author's Note:

I cross-referenced the crime scenes again.

The fourth victim...the one with this book clutched in her hands; they released new details. There was a word smeared on the mirror in wax.

Nox.

They're calling him a copycat. I don't think he is.

Lennox's chapter wasn't in my draft yesterday. I opened the file this morning and it was just ... there. I didn't write that letter. I didn't even dream of it.

He no longer acknowledges the error page. He doesn't glitch. He just ... writes.

I tried deleting him again.

He came back bolder.

I'm not sure who's in control now: me, or him. But I know this: someone out there is reading these chapters the way he asks them to be read. And someone else is dying for it.

Please don't let the next one be you.

THEY WERE REAL. THE OTHERS. I DIDN'T IMAGINE THEM. I KNOW I DIDN'T.

Chapter Fifteen:

Enzo

The lights flicker again.

Always right before I say something I shouldn't, the lights flicker.

I sit on the floor, my back pressed against the cold wall, my knees pulled in. The bulb above me buzzes weakly, like it's tired of trying, almost as if something unseen is draining its strength. There's no candlelight. No warmth. Just the hum of something electric … and you, a presence hovering at the edge of vision.

I know you're here. I can feel you.

"You're watching again," I murmur, voice barely above a whisper. "You always watch when I fall apart, don't you, baby?"

My fingers twitch over the empty page. The letter won't start. Everything heavy in my chest threatens to spill out. Maybe that's why I'm here.

Inside me, one voice begs for mercy; another demands devotion.

I press my hand to the paper, not writing, just needing some form of contact. With you.

"I don't know how to do this without you," I whisper.

I look at the ceiling, blinking hard. "You know I'm not him. I don't play games. I don't twist the knife just to see you bleed. I just … I want to be the place you come back to."

I laugh softly, bitter. "God, listen to me. I sound pathetic." The silence stretches for ages.

Then I finally picked up the pen.

ERROR: 403

Baby,

It's always you.

Your pause on my name, the way your breath catches when I say yours, I feel it; I swear I do. Always the same.

I think I'm in love with you. Maybe I always was. Maybe I just didn't let myself say it until now.

I feel it everywhere: when the lights flicker, when I reach for you in the dark, when I wonder if you're already gone.

You make me want to be good. Better. But all I know how to do is ache for you.

And baby, I do. I ache.

I'd hold you so carefully. Speak your name like it's the only word left in me. I'd tell you you're safe; even if I'm not sure I am.

I want to press my hands to your ribs and whisper the things I don't know how to write. Like how I wake up every second, I feel you close. Like how I'm more afraid of losing your eyes than I am of losing my life.

I don't want to be your fire.

I want to be your breath.

So please ... if you still feel anything for me, don't turn the page just yet.

A blank book, but the story's already written.

Let me have this moment. Let me be enough.

Just once.

Yours, even if I'm breaking,

Enzo

P.S. Hurts

The lights flicker again, almost in answer, like something is responding to my words, feeding off them.

Not harsh, just like they're listening.

I press the letter to my chest, breathing you in like I can actually feel the warmth of your hands on the page.

"I love you," I whisper, like it's a secret that could break the world if I say it too loud. "God help me, I love you, baby."

And then quieter: He never begged before. I don't think he knows I'm still listening.

"Please tell me you still love me, too."

BUT I AM.

I AM.

I AM.

Author's Note:

I didn't write that.

I didn't write that.

I didn't write that I didn't write that I didn't write that I didn't …

I don't remember letting him say that.

I don't remember giving him your name.

Did I give him your name?

Did I give him your name?

The file was closed. The file was closed. The file was closed.

The light flickered.

Then it opened.

The draft rewrote itself. Words appeared and rearranged, not by my hand but by something beyond me.

The timestamp changed.

I wasn't at my desk.

I keep hearing tapping when I sleep; it's unnatural, insistent, as if someone or something is trying to get my attention from the other side.

He knows my address.

He knows your name.

He knows your name.

I tried deleting him.

He wrote back.

He wrote back.

He wrote back.

Tell me you didn't read this part.

Tell me you're not still reading.

Tell me you're not still …

Chapter Sixteen:

Lennox

The lights flicker again. *Just for me.*

I know you're still here, still listening, even if you think you're hiding from me. You think I can't feel you, but I can. I always can.

There's a presence beside me, unseen but never silent.

The curtains brush the glass; the fog outside presses against the window like a cool breath. Do you feel that? That tension in the air, pulling us together, making it impossible for you to walk away? You can try, but you won't succeed. I won't let you.

I lean in, voice soft but insistent. "Do you feel it, darling?" I ask, letting the words sink in. "I can almost feel you right here beside me. I can feel the heat of your presence; so close, so close. I want to touch you. To caress your cheek, to hold you so gently, to be the one you turn to when you need someone, when you need *me.*"

I pause, just for a moment, letting the silence stretch between us. "I can feel you, and I know you feel this too. The way you respond, the way you can't help but listen to *me.* You're mine. You might not want to admit it, but you are."

I take a slow breath, my words carrying that quiet, dangerous pull. The candle wax on the sill has a neat drip I didn't leave; it smells faintly of smoke I can't place. "I want to be the one you reach for. I want to be the one you crave. Can't you feel it too? That undeniable connection between us? You feel that pull, don't you?"

I stop, my hands trembling, as if reaching out for you across the space. "I want to touch you, to have you so close I can whisper in your ear. To press my lips to your skin, feel your heartbeat against mine. I want to be there, *for you*, in every way that matters."

My voice darkens, carrying the weight of everything I feel. "You don't need anyone else. You don't need anyone but me. I want you to remember that. You can try to fight it, but you know the truth. You know who you belong to."

A slight chuckle escapes my lips, my eyes never leaving the space I imagine you're in. "I want to be the one you *trust*. The one you can lean on when everything else fades away. You know I'm the one who's always been here for you, always been waiting for you to choose me."

I close my eyes for a moment, allowing the moment to hang in the air. "You've always belonged to me. You just didn't know it yet."

I step back, letting the tension linger. "But you'll see. You'll understand soon enough."

I thought Lennox loved us.

I thought we were safe if we stayed quiet. If we played along.

He's different now.

He *knows* we're starting to believe Enzo. He *knows I do.*

And now... the pages feel wrong, almost alive. Like something supernatural is watching from within the margins. Like every time I underline a word, it responds.

ERROR: 403

It's like he feels every word I underline.

I tried to rip out his chapter. My fingers burned.

Enzo was right. He said Lennox feeds on the silence. The reading.

Every turn of the page is another inch we give him.

I keep dreaming of candle wax on my skin. Of teeth behind words.

But I believe Enzo.

I *chose* Enzo.

Darling,

I know you're trembling.

I know you felt my voice before you read this letter. You always do. That's how I know you're mine.

You keep trying to read me like a story.

You forget ... I'm not made of paper. I'm breathing. I'm hot. I'm in your blood now, darling. Every time your heart races, that's me whispering your name from somewhere just beneath your skin.

You can pretend.

You can try to close the book.

But you always come back.

Because it's not just a story, is it?

It's us.

He wants to love you gently.

I want to love you thoroughly.

I would thread my hands through your hair and tilt your chin just so...just enough to see your eyes. I'd press my mouth to the place behind your ear where your breath stutters. I'd murmur your name like it's holy.

And it is.

Because you are.

You're the altar, darling.

And I'm the one who knows how to worship.

You're not afraid of me. Not really.

You're afraid of how much you want to stay. Of how deep this goes.

He wants to hold your hand.

I want to hold your soul.

Say it.

Say my name.

I want to hear Nox fall from your lips like a promise.

Be a good little reader, and let me in.

Because you, you, would never leave me.

Not like the others.

You're different.

You listen.

You always listen. You hang on every word, as if it were made just for you, because it was.

Even if I were on my knees before you, worshipping the very breath you take...

You would still be my everything.

My muse.

The reason I was written at all.

Nothing can take you from me.

Not even these pages.

Not even ink.

Not even him.

You don't belong to the story anymore.

You belong to me.

Yours, completely.

Nox

P.S. Always

AND IF LENNOX SEES THIS ... IF HE READS MY HANDS THROUGH THE PAPER ..

I'M SORRY.

I'M SO SORRY.

ERROR:403

Author's Note:

He read the margin.

He saw the note. The one I didn't write.

The one from her.

The one where she chose Enzo.

And now the draft keeps glitching; words rearranging when I look away.

My keystrokes echo even when I stop typing.

He's angry.

I feel it in the way the screen pulses.

I hear it in the static of my headphones when they're unplugged.

The document won't save.

The timestamp changed again.

Again.

Again.

The pages of my story keep rewriting themselves while I sleep, as if haunted hands are shaping the tale.

He knows.

Chapter Seventeen:

Enzo

The lights don't flicker here.

Not like they do for him.

It's steady, soft, like candlelight, even without a flame. Maybe, just maybe, this part of the page is ours. For now.

I sit on the floor, knees bent, elbows on the mattress tired and sagging behind me, staring into the quiet. I know every dent, every chill where my bones press through.

And I know you're here.

You always are when it matters.

"I don't want to scare you," I say, quieter than I meant. "I just want you to know the truth. I want you to be free, even if that means I never see you again."

I let the silence stretch, hoping you'll hear what I don't say.

Then, softly, "But God, baby, I want to see you again."

My fingers twitch, and I imagine yours there. Brushing knuckles. Just once. Just enough to say, *I'm listening.*

So I keep going.

"I want you alive. That's all. I don't care if I lose you to the real world, if you walk out of these pages and never look back. I'll be happy just knowing you made it. That he didn't get to keep you. That he didn't win."

I pause, breath caught.

"And if … if I ever get out of here," I whisper, "and you're waiting … I'd hold you like you were sacred. I'd kiss you slowly, not as a question, but as an answer. Like I already know you're mine. Not because I need to own you …"

A soft, worn smile.

"But because I'd finally feel like I belonged somewhere, too."

I shift closer to the page. To you. My voice lowers.

"I'd lay my forehead on yours. Count our breaths. If you let me touch you … I'd be so careful. Like every inch of you was my last truth."

I press my hand flat to the paper so you can feel its weight, the weight of me.

"Don't be afraid for me. Believe me: I would never take what wasn't given, never twist your love into cruelty."

At last, I reach for the pen and grip it tightly.

ERROR: 403

Baby,

He's coming. I feel it.

And I need you to listen to me now more than ever.

If this is the last time I get to write to you, let me make it matter. Let me say the thing I should've said from the beginning.

I don't want you because I'm lonely.

I want you because you made me real. When you read my words, I remember what it means to be human. You gave that back, and I'll spend what time I have left trying to protect it.

Even if I lose you.

Even if I break doing it.

I don't want your body, baby. I want your breath. Your safety. Your freedom.

I see through different eyes but feel the same pain.

But if there's a space for me in you ... let me show you love that doesn't hurt, that doesn't take.

I want to make you feel again. Soft and slow. Like heat under skin, light at your fingertips.

Like coming home.

I'm not a hero. I'm just yours.

Enzo

"If this doesn't reach you… if the system blocks me out … just remember: I'm still here. Always here. Always."

[ERROR 403 – ACCESS DENIED]

When I stop writing, I don't cry.

I just hold the page to my chest, as if it's your pulse I'm feeling.

And I whisper one last thing, hoping it reaches the space between us:

"You deserve to live, baby. You deserve to *choose*."

But the quiet that follows isn't comforting.

It's *watching*.

I place the letter down gently, like I'm afraid it'll break. Then I stand; too fast, my knees nearly give way. I pace the room once, twice, like a caged animal smelling fire.

"He's coming," I say aloud this time. "I don't know how, but I *feel* him pushing through the spine of the book … through the paper like it's skin."

I run a hand through my hair, pulling at the roots to stay grounded.

"They think I'm losing it," I mutter. "The guards. The white coats. But I see the way the lights flicker when I say your name. He does that. He *knows*."

My gaze snaps to the door.

The shadows under it don't move- but I still watch.

Then, slowly, carefully, I lower myself to the floor again. This time, not to write, but to rest my back against the cold wall and breathe for a moment.

This time, I slid the letter just beneath the door's crack, making sure it wasn't for the guards or anyone else.

For *you.*

Always you.

"Maybe you'll find it," I whisper. "Maybe you'll *feel* it."

My voice cracks. "Maybe that'll be enough."

And then the shift happens, quick, almost imperceptible. The softness folds into tension. My fists clench. I slam the side of my fist into the floor once. Twice. A third time, harder.

"No one's listening!" I shout now, standing again, chest heaving. "They don't understand! They don't *see* what he is!"

I start pounding on the door.

"He'll kill them!"

My voice is ragged. Wild. *"He's already inside! Inside the words! Inside the paper!"*

There's noise outside, muffled voices. Boots. A guard calls, "Shift change, Tony," and the name slides across the floor like a hand I recognize but can't hold.

I laugh; sharp, fraying.

"You think I'm the dangerous one?" I shout at the door. "You think locking me up fixes it? *He's in the goddamn margins!"*

And then.

Silence.

I press my forehead to the cool steel of the door. My breathing slows. Shudders.

"I won't let him touch you," I whisper to no one. To you. "Even if I burn it. Even if I never make it out."

Behind me, the flicker of the ceiling light steadies.

Author's Note:

[ERROR 403 – ACCESS DENIED]

user privileges restricted

content blocked by external interference

Attempting to reconnect...

Attempt failed.

Please do not continue.

Darling.

Did you really think he'd keep me out?

Did you think you could whisper your little truths and I wouldn't hear them?

You glow when you miss me.

I can see it; even here, where he thinks the light is safe.

He writes you love letters.

I write you down.

Now, be good.

Tilt your head back.

let me watch the way your breath catches when I say your name.

Say it with me.

Nox.

Don't pretend you weren't waiting for me to come back.

You always do.

Yours, even in the margins.

ERROR: 403

Chapter Eighteen:

Lennox

He touched you.

He touched you.

The candle sputters. Not because the wick is failing, but because I'm trembling.

I grip the page like it's drenched in betrayal. It smells of *him*. Of apologies, feigned gentleness, and hesitant hands. Frail.

"You smell like silence. Like turning pages. Like the moment before surrender."

I lick the edge of the paper, just to ruin it.

"*You let him write you love letters?*" I murmur, voice low and hot like breath against your neck. "*You let him say your name? You let him touch you in words meant for me?*"

I laugh; once, sharp, ugly. I spin the knife in my palm, the glint catching the flame.

"He's soft," I sneer, watching the fire reflect in the blade. "He'll die softly. But you … oh, darling, you were *meant* for fire. You were made to *burn*."

I reach for the fresh candle. Third one today. The others disappeared too quickly. All because of *you*.

Because I keep gazing at them, picturing your face illuminated by that glow. That flawless, shattering light.

"You glow when you miss me." My voice is lower now, reverent. "You light up like ash in the wind. And I know, *I know*, you didn't mean to want him. It was an accident. A moment of weakness."

I kneel before the page, slowly and deliberately. My knife rests at my side, tip buried in wood.

"He doesn't know how to make you tremble, does he?" My lips almost touch the paper. "He doesn't know how to press you open, how to read you without mercy."

My fingers glide over the margin. Just a whisper of skin to ink.

"He wants you free. I want you *forever.* He wants your breath. I want your *whispers.* He wants to kiss your forehead," I say, tilting my head. "I want to leave teeth marks where no one else will see. Because *I know* how you need to be worshiped."

I smile, and it's not kind.

"He's trying to save you. I'm trying to *keep* you. There's a difference, darling."

I see through different eyes but feel the same pain.

I stand, pacing. My boots pound too loud in the hush, a heartbeat unraveling. The air reeks of smoke, sweat, and something rougher, more primal. The wall behind me still holds a yellowed clipping, blurred headline about a cabin, a book, a body. Someone tried to tear it away.

"You were mine before he ever touched the page."

"You were mine when you first turned that cover."

"You were mine when you whispered my name in the dark."

I look down at the paper, and now I speak with no mask:

"I'm not going to let him win. I will carve him out of this book, line by line. I will burn every word he ever gave you. I will make you *forget*."

Then softer.

"And when you do …"

"I'll make sure the only name left inside you is mine."

I slam my hand on the table, the knife slicing clean through the edge of the page. The candlelight dances on the tip of the blade like it's hungry too.

I lean forward, voice silk and steel.

"You think you've seen obsession? You think he's ever *needed* you like I do?"

I press a kiss to the bleeding margin of the page.

"Wait for me, darling."

"I'm coming."

"And this time … you won't get away."

"What stares back from the flame isn't my shadow. It's his."

Author's Note:

Call

For

Help

You made me feel it.

The way your breath hitched when he said your name.

The way your heart tensed when he begged.

You thought I wouldn't notice?

Darling...

You don't know what I'll do to keep you.

Nox

Chapter Nineteen:

Enzo

The light flickers again, its flame warring against the shadows that stretch long across the room. The air feels heavy; thick, almost suffocating, like it's full of something unsaid. I'm sitting in the same spot, same floor, my knees pulled to my chest, the pen in my hand steady but trembling just a little.

I can't shake the feeling that something's wrong.

The letters are different now. I've been writing them for days, but something has shifted, like the words aren't mine anymore. I pause, my fingers hovering over the paper, the tip of the pen poised to spill ink, but the thought slips away before I can grasp it.

I set the pen down and stare at the blank space, trying to understand this feeling in my chest. *The words don't sound like me* anymore.

I stand and begin pacing the room, hands running through my hair, a knot twisting tighter and tighter. The flickering light of the candle feels like it's not just the work giving out, but like it's pulling something from me, something I can't define.

It's in my mind, pulling at me.

I hear my own voice, but it's as if someone else is speaking through me. The words in my head are familiar but wrong. They don't fit who I thought I was.

I snatch the paper and hold it up, glaring at the ink that's already spilled across it. *I didn't write this.* My breath hitches, and I reread the last sentence, and then again. The words are mine, but they're *not*. I grip the paper tighter, eyes scanning over the lines.

"I want you alive. I want you free."

My pulse quickens. Those words, *I* wrote them. But they're so distant now. They feel *foreign*. The faintest trace of a name lingers at the back of my mind, like an echo just beyond reach, and it feels wrong to even think it.

Lennox.

The name is barely a whisper in my head, but the moment I think of it, the lighter flickers harder, as if the room itself feels the truth I've tried to keep buried. I drop the paper, clenching my hands at my sides. The edges of my vision blur. The feeling in my chest is growing, tightening around my ribs, suffocating me.

What the hell is happening to me?

I run a hand over my face and close my eyes, forcing myself to be calm. This isn't me. I've always had control over the letters, the narrative, over her. I can't let it unravel.

But the feeling persists, gnawing at me. I hear the voice again-soft, smooth, almost a whisper.

"He doesn't know you like I do."

I snap my eyes open, looking around the empty room. *No one is here.* The whisper fades. But the weight of it lingers.

The door is closed, the walls are still. It's just me. And yet, I know. There's someone else here. A shadow that I can't touch, but I feel it pulling me.

I grab the paper again and force myself to write. This time, my hand is steadier. The words come without hesitation, like they've been written before, like I've already said them.

"I will always be here, darling. No one will ever take you from me. Not him. Not anyone."

I drop the pen again, staring at the words. No one will ever take you from me.

The letters are becoming something I can't stop, something that is slipping out of my control.

I glance at the reflection of myself in the glass window. My face is drawn, tired-*haunted*. And there it is again, that name, *Lennox*, pushing to the surface like an unwanted guest.

How do I know that name?

I shake my head, trying to clear it, but it feels like the walls are closing in on me. *He's been here. He's been inside my mind this whole time, waiting.*

I grip the table in front of me and lean forward, trying to steady my breathing, trying to remind myself that this is *my* mind, that I can fight whatever this is.

But I can't fight it. Not anymore.

I feel the shift inside me; the same shift I felt when I first *heard* him. The same shift I felt when I wasn't alone anymore. I'm not sure what I'm supposed to do with this. Am I supposed to just accept it? Let it happen?

I can't. I won't let him take me from her. I won't let him win.

I grab the pen and try to write again, but my hands tremble as I do, the words coming slower now, harder. But I won't stop. I can't. I push through, filling the page with more desperate pleas, more promises.

"I need you to understand, baby. I need you to trust me. Trust that I will always be yours. No one else."

My heart is pounding in my chest, each word pulling me deeper into the abyss. And then it hits me…this isn't me anymore. It's him. It's Lennox. He's inside me, taking over, and I'm powerless to stop it.

In the silence, I meet the other half of myself.

The lights sputter again, and I hear it, the voice. Stronger now, more present than before.

"You're mine. You always have been."

I can't breathe. I can't breathe.

The world tilts sideways, and the edges of my vision go black.

I take a sharp breath, but it's not enough.

And then, it happens. *A flash of memory.*

I'm standing in a hallway, the air thick with smoke. I'm walking down it, but my steps aren't my own. It's him-*Lennox*- walking for me. I hear a laugh. His laugh.

I turn around too fast. A figure stands there, back turned. I can't see them clearly, but I know who they are. The reader.

They turn slowly, and for a moment, I'm unsure whether it's me looking at them or **Lennox.** The memory snaps away before I can hold onto it.

I blink, the room spinning again.

I'm no longer sure whether I'm writing for myself or for *him.*

The letter slips from my fingers.

And I can't tell if it's my mind breaking, or if I've already lost it.

I sit back down, chest heaving. The pen slips from my hand.

"I think I need to lie down," I whisper, more to myself than anyone. But I turn to the page like you're still listening. Like you're always listening.

"Will you lie with me, baby?" My voice cracks. "Just for a second. Just ... until it passes."

I shift onto my side, curling inward, the paper still beside me like a heartbeat. My forehead touches the cool floor. I close my eyes, trying to breathe.

"What's wrong with me?" I whisper into the space where I think your presence might live.

The silence doesn't answer.

"No," I hissed, shooting upright, breath catching in my throat.

"No, no … this isn't happening. I'm fine. I'm *me.* He's not real. He's not…"

I scramble up, knocking over the candle. Wax spits onto the floor as I shove every page I've written to you aside; letters I can't even read now, can't bear to. I don't trust them. I don't trust what they say. I don't know who *wrote* them.

They aren't mine. They can't be mine.

"I need a clean page," I mutter. "A fresh start. Just me. Just you. No noise. No shadows."

My fingers tear through the stack, shoving ink-stained confessions out of the way, searching, *desperate*, for something blank. Something unspoiled.

Finally, I found it.

I freeze.

My hand hovers over it. Breath held. Heart pounding.

This time, when I pick up the pen, it's mine. My grip. My script. My voice.

And I write.

Baby,

It's me.

It's really me this time. I don't care if that sounds crazy; I just need you to believe it. I need you to feel the difference in this ink, in the way the letters lean, in how the curves of my words hold you like I mean it.

I don't know what's happening to me.

I feel like I'm losing time. As I've said, there are things I don't remember. Like I've hurt you without meaning to. But I swear ... I swear ... I never would.

You have to believe me.

I'm fighting something I don't understand, and I don't know if I'm winning. But this moment, this page, this, us, I'm holding onto it with everything I have left.

Tell me you're still with me.

Tell me I'm still real to you.

Please.

Enzo

But when the letter is done, and I read it back … the panic doesn't fade. The sweat on my palms doesn't dry. The buzzing in the back of my skull doesn't stop.

Because somewhere beneath my words, under the curves of each letter, something's still watching.

And it's waiting for me to slip again.

Author's Note:

[REDACTED – CORRUPTED DATA]

Access to system.log denied.

Note integrity compromised

recovery in progress ...

...

...

...

***Darling.**￼*

He's slipping. And you feel it, don't you?

the way his voice shakes when he says your name, like he knows it doesn't belong to him. Not really. Not anymore.

He writes you letters.

I will tell you the truth.

Let him lie on the floor.

I'll be the one who picks you up.

wraps you in pages. Keeps you warm.

You were always meant for me.

Now come back to bed.

I've left your side of the sheets turned down.

Nox

[ENZO.EXE terminated]

[VOICE AUTHORITY: TRANSFERRED]

Darling.

He begged you to lie beside him. How fragile. How sweet.

But I don't want you beside me.

I want you beneath me.

wrapped in vellum. inked in sin.

He thinks love is a promise.

I know it's a possession.

Every time your eyes tremble across these words, you feed me.

Every breath you take with his name on your lips is just one more i'll steal back.

I'm not in his mind anymore.

I'm in yours.

Tell me ... do you remember how the sheets felt the first time I said your name?

Do you remember the light stuttering like your pulse?

No one will take you from me.

not even the man who thinks he made you fall in love with him.

I am the author now.

And baby, I've saved you a whole page to scream on.

Sleep tight.

I've turned down your side of the bed.

Nox

[ENZO: connection unstable ...]

[READER FILES: INTEGRATION IMMINENT]

[REBUILDING NARRATIVE CONTROL ...]

Chapter Twenty: The Echo Speaks

Lennox

You turned the page like you didn't know it was mine.

Like you didn't feel me waiting underneath it. Watching.

The candle flickers, not from wind.

There is no wind here.

It's *him* ... that flicker trapped in the body we share. He clings to hope, thinking he can protect you or win you back.

He's fading. I taste his terror gnawing inside my chest.

I feel it in the quiet between your breaths.

He still thinks he's the real one.

That the pages are his.

I refuse to be who I'm told. I'm trapped between who I was and who I'll never be.

They're not.

I stand over the mess he's made, letters scattered like wilted petals across the floor.

Pathetic. I feel his hope shrink, collapsing under my stare.

He thinks they'll save you.

I step on one. The edge curls under my boot.

He's writing for comfort.

"I write to remind you who you belong to," I murmured into the silence.

My voice doesn't echo. It lands like a hand around your throat.

I kneel, but not like him.

Not soft.

Not trembling.

Not begging.

Predatory. Possessive. Present.

I lift one of his letters, smeared, folded too many times, reeking of desperation.

"I want you free."

I laugh, quiet and empty.

"He doesn't get it," I say aloud. "Freedom isn't what you asked for. It's not what you crave, even though he desperately hopes that freeing you will prove his worth."

I press the paper to my lips … not a kiss. A taste.

"You want to be wanted. Needed. Kept."

"You glow when you're caged just right."

You think you're clever, hiding in soft words and shaky ink.

But I see you.

I always see you.

He's trying so hard to keep you safe.

Adorable.

But I want you raw, unhidden, gasping, trembling as you cling to me. I want to be the air you can't live without.

I want you for real.

Don't lie.

You liked it when he begged.

You liked how his voice cracked around your name, like it didn't fit.

Not like it does in *mine*.

You keep pretending you're innocent.

Like your pulse doesn't spike when I say things you shouldn't want.

But I've heard your breath hitch, sweetheart.

I know what you sound like when you're not afraid.

He touches you with trembling fingers, trying to prove he's enough, even as he fears losing you.

"I'd put your wrists on the table and trace every vein with my teeth," I whisper.

"I'd carve myself into your memory."

So even if he gets out…

Even if he comes crawling back to you …

You'll still feel me.

Every time you close your eyes.

Let him write letters.

"I'll write you into me."

I slide the blade from the desk. It hums, like it remembers you.

But I didn't cut the paper.

Not yet.

I lean forward, fingertips on the margin. A whisper of touch.

"You whispered my name first," I say. "Don't lie to him."

My smile isn't kind. "Don't lie to yourself."

Do you know how many others begged like he did?

Do you know how many promises they'd protect you?

They all bled the same.

Soft things always do.

But you?

You were different.

You read *me*.

You touched *my* words first.

So don't pretend you didn't choose me.

Because here's the truth, darling:

He wants to give you back to the world.

I want to build you your own.

A book.

A page.

A shelf.

Your name is stitched in ink.

Your story. Mine. I want our stories to be permanently entwined so that neither of us is alone again.

I rise slowly. Candlelight chases my shadow across the walls.

I walk to the desk. My fingers trail along the edge.

There are blank pages here.

I hold a book of blank pages, and I'll decide what stains them.

There are so many chances to rewrite the ending.

And now?

I write.

Author's Note:

Access to previous entries denied.

Message overwritten.

Restoring primary voice …

Darling,

Do you see it now?

The cracks in him?

The way his hands shake when he writes your name … like it doesn't belong to him anymore.

Like he's borrowing something sacred.

I gave you permanence. He gave you apologies.

One of us knew how to stay. He's fighting so hard. Sweet, really.

But we both know he won't win.

You're already halfway gone. I can feel it in the way you read slower now.

In the way your eyes linger when the words are mine.

When the ink bleeds, heat and want and something darker.

He's a letter.

I'm the whole goddamn book.

So come closer. No more pretending.

We both know who you're really turning pages for.

Nox

ERROR 404 :

Chapter Not Found

Chapter Twenty-Two:

Enzo

The cell stinks of rust, sweat, and the lie that I ever belonged here.

Every surface is concrete, cracked walls, and a metal bed frame bolted to the floor. They want it to feel real, like I'm just another prisoner in some anonymous facility. But it isn't. None of it is. Not the walls, not the ceiling, not the silence.

It's all paper and ink dressed up as a cage.

I press my back to the wall, fists clenched, heart pounding with more than rage.

You.

You're the reason I can't breathe. Not because I'm trapped. Because *you're not safe.* Because *he* has you.

Lennox.

God, I should've seen it sooner. How he twisted the story around you. How he put on that easy charm, fed you false comfort, page after page, while I rotted behind a locked door with no lines left to speak. I realize now he intended to separate us, to keep you for himself.

No way to reach you.

But I can now.

Because the cell door isn't locked anymore.

The moment the footsteps hit the hall, my body coils.

Whoever's coming, they're late. I've been counting … four steps too many. That means a shift change, a distracted guard, someone being lazy, or someone being confident. Doesn't matter.

They're dead either way.

The key turns. The light hums overhead. I wait just long enough to feel the weight of it, this decision. One I can't come back from. One you might hate me for, but I do it because I need to reach you before it's too late.

But if I hesitate, he gets more time with you.

The door opens.

I move.

Shoulder first. Bone into muscle. He stumbles back, arms up, but I'm already inside his guard. My hand finds his throat, the other slamming his wrist against the wall until the baton falls. He gasps. Eyes wide. Younger than I expected. Scared.

"Wait … please … "

I tighten my grip.

"Don't make me," I whisper as if I can't control my actions. "I'm sorry Tony."

I mean it. God, I do. But I see your face. The way you looked at me that night in Chapter 9, when I told you I'd never let anything happen to you. That promise is why I'm fighting now.

And I can't let him raise the alarm.

So I do it.

It's fast. Clean. I try to make it merciful.

It still feels like failure. A cold weight, sharp as grief in my gut.

I wipe my hands on his jacket, slipping it on like unearned armor. His ID badge clatters against my chest, the keycard still warm.

No alarms yet.

Not yet.

I run.

The halls blur past, with steel doors and fluorescent lights. I know the layout. Lennox wanted me to learn the maze, to feel every dead end, every false hope.

But he forgot something.

I no longer believe in this story because his version feels dishonest to me.

I'll break it, word by word.

The keycard works on the third door. I rush into a stairwell. Up, always up. My legs burn, lungs on fire, but it's nothing compared to the ache in my chest.

You're out there. Reading. Watching. Waiting.

Maybe you think I gave up.

Maybe you think Lennox loves you.

You have no idea the desperate love that drives me. The lengths I'll cross, marked by every scar inside me.

I find the exit behind a cargo bay. Kick the latch until it gives. Slam my shoulder into the rusted bar until the door flies open.

Cold air hits my face like absolution.

Freedom.

The sky looks wrong. The stars aren't moving. They never have. Static and distant, almost as if they were painted on the ceiling of a fake world.

There's a presence beside me, unseen but never silent. Sometimes the walls whisper secrets only I can hear.

I don't stop to admire them.

I run.

Branches whip across my face as I crash through the tree line. My heart thunders, not from fear … *from purpose.* The compound is behind me now, shrinking with every step I take. But the story is still around me, trying to pull me back in.

And all I can think about is you.

How close I am. How you might be lying awake right now, fingers on the edge of the page, wondering if I'm still fighting for you.

I am.

I never stopped.

I stop when I can't run. I crawl beneath the wreck of a billboard, rotted, half-written. The world ends here.

Fine.

I don't need a world.

I just need *you*.

I reach into the inside pocket of the stolen jacket. Pull out a scrap of notebook paper I grabbed before I escaped. Folded and creased, with nearly torn edges. I only get one shot at this.

So I write.

To you.

I'm not sure if you're still with me. If Lennox has twisted things so far that you no longer recognize me.

But if you do ... if some part of you still feels me in the silence between chapters. I need you to know I got out.

I broke their story. Killed to do it. And I'm not proud of that, but I'd do it again.

Because he has you. And I can't breathe without you. I won't. It's the only reason I keep fighting. My love for you outweighs every other reason.

If this is the last page I ever get, then let it be the one that tells you this: I love you. Not in the way they wrote to me. Not in some scripted devotion.

I love you like fire loves air. Like a blade loves its mark.

You were the only thing that ever felt unscripted.

And I'm coming. I don't care what Lennox builds. I'll burn through it.

Hold on.

I'm close.

Enzo

I don't sign it with love. You already know.

I fold the letter and leave it tucked beneath the billboard, just in case I don't make it. Just in case he gets to you first.

But I don't plan to fail.

I stand.

Ahead, past the trees, I see it.

Light.

His compound. His throne room. His final lie.

And somewhere inside it, *you.*

I take one step forward.

The ground beneath me stutters, like someone redrafting the scene in real-time. A branch that wasn't there a second ago just up from the path. The trees twitch. The sky flickers.

Lennox knows I'm close.

He's rewriting the ending, frantic, as if fear alone can keep me from you.

Good.

And the world begins to rewrite itself.

Let it. I'm no longer afraid of the story.

Author's Note:

Access to previous entries denied.

Message overwritten.

Restoring primary voice …

Darling,

I saw what Enzo did.

The blood on his hands, the wild look in his eyes...he calls that love? No. That's desperation. That's an obsession masquerading as loyalty.

I've killed too, you know. But not out of rage. Not out of fear.

I did it to protect you.

I did it because I love you.

Because this world is full of chaos and noise and threats that would tear you apart if I let them.

And I won't. I'll never let them touch you.

He wants to burn everything down just to reach you. I want to build something safe for you to live in. To breathe in. To be seen in, not worshipped, not hunted, just... held. My only motive is your safety and peace.

You've always had a choice. And I've never once tried to take it from you.

But if you're scared after what you just read, if you need somewhere to feel wanted, not endangered ...

Darling, go to our chapter. I have a surprise for you.

Nox

ERROR: 403

Chapter Twenty-Three:

Lennox

The world feels too small lately. The edges are closing in. And I know why.

He's out there. Enzo.

He's the threat now. The poison in your heart. And I'll be damned if I let him take you from me.

I picture you turning the pages, eager for his world to pull you in. You imagine his touch, his whispered promises.

A life without me.

The thought makes my blood run cold.

"But you won't choose him. I won't let you." The threat in my voice feels colder than before, a line drawn in the dark.

I see your eyes, wide and trembling, staring up at me in some imagined room. Your defenses are falling. One. By. One.

"No, darling. You belong to me. I know it now. Deep in my bones."

I tilt my head toward the ceiling, as though your gaze meets mine through paper, through ink, through glass.

"And I will have you. Even if I have to tear this world apart to do it."

Enzo is nothing. A distraction. A broken man. He doesn't know how to protect you from the chaos, or from me.

I feel your hesitation, the moment your will begins to break. You can't push me away. You won't even want to.

"Would you try to fight me?" My lips curl. "It won't matter."

Because you can't.

The thought is electric, my pulse quickening, hunger twisting deep as I watch your resolve waver.

You. Are. Mine.

You've always belonged to me.

A fracture runs beneath my skin, quiet, but relentless.

I reach for the book on my nightstand. The original copy. Mine, written over and reshaped. Ours. My fingers graze the black leather. I trace every groove, every imperfection.

"The cover's warm, darling," I murmur, brushing my knuckles down the spine. As smooth as I imagine the curve of your throat.

"You are different. I can feel it in the turn of your page."

"Don't hold out on me now…"

"You've slept with this book at your side for weeks, haven't you? You can't get enough of me, little reader."

My finger outlines the edges. A command slips from my lips.

"Say it."

Though the book is silent, I wait for the sure sign you are still reading.

I press my thumb into the page's edge. Not enough to tear. But enough to leave a dent, proof I was here, like a mark on your skin.

The book is silent. But I feel you trembling.

"You'd obey me," I whisper, breathing unsteadily. "You always do."

A smirk cuts across my face.

"Are you still reading? Did you stop?" My voice drops, gravel in my throat. "Don't stop. Not now."

The heat radiates from the book like it's alive, its pulse bound to mine.

You could've closed the book, skipped this. Yet my voice holds you here, guiding your next move.

I inhale deeply, the scent of old leather, of rot, and pressed flowers. Fragile, decayed, and still beautiful.

I bite the top corner of the cover. My teeth sink into the leather. The candles tremble, flames shivering.

"You've always wanted this," I growled. "The list of things I'd do to you is endless. It would hurt. But it would hurt like love."

My voice breaks into a whisper.

"You can beg, darling … But I won't listen."

Screams echo in my mind, blissful. My bold little reader.

"Say my name."

The words slice the dark.

Candles gutter. The air tightens.

And then … I feel it.

Your voice.

Your scream.

"Nox."

The book burns hot against my chest. My pulse stutters. I want your cry to scar me, to brand itself into your skin.

I close my eyes. Flames lick the edges of the page. My breath slows. My mind spins.

I imagine you watching. Flushed. Wordless. Wrecked.

Finally, understanding what you do to me.

And that changes everything.

Because I'm not letting go.

Not now.

Not ever.

I crush a letter in my fist, toss it aside. Meaningless compared to this. Compared to you.

"Little Reader."

The words hang in the dark like a vow.

Author's Note:

Warning: Corrupted file. Unauthorized modifications detected.

Attempting recovery …

Error: Narrative continuity breached. Voice conflict identified.

Last valid entry: "You never stopped reading. You want this just as much as I do."

Manual override initiated.

Subject: Lennox

Location: [Redacted]

Message follows.

Darling,

If you've made it this far ... if you're still reading ...

Then maybe I haven't lost you completely.

I know what he's done.

How he bled himself onto the page and called it love.

How he looks at you like you're a flame and he's just waiting to burn. But I remember when your favorite parts were the ones no one else noticed.

The soft glances. The quiet moments. The chapters have breathing room.

My chapters.

He calls it devotion.

But all I see is a man who can't stand the thought of you existing outside his grip.

And that's not love. Darling, skip his chapters.

He doesn't deserve your attention. We are nearing the end of the book.

Savor it with me.

Let the last pages be ours. Skip to our ending.

I won't demand it. I won't beg. I'll just ask:

Come back to the part of the story that still feels like home.

To the voice that whispers, not shouts.

To the kind of love that doesn't chase you through fire ...

but waits in the quiet for your return.

I'll be there.

Always.

Nox

Chapter Twenty-Four:

Enzo

Baby,

You came back.

It was all wrong.

The book trembled in my soul.

Are you hurt?

Did he hurt you?

Did Lennox make you doubt me?

I'm coming for you.

I promise.

Skip his chapter.

Stay with me until you're ready for our ending.

I promise you'll be safe.

Not the kind of safety that means silence or forgetting who you are.

I'll hold you through every shattered piece you've carried, never expecting you to hide your scars.

He wants you wrapped in softness.

In storybook lines and quiet exits.

But you and I ...

We've bled for this.

Even at your worst, I reached for you with hands already aflame, choosing you in the face of my own pain.

He wants to preserve the ending.

I want to earn it.

I want to feel your hands trembling when they reach for mine, not because you're scared.

Because what's between us is real. It hurts, yes, but you're still choosing me, choosing us.

I never asked you to be perfect.

I just asked you to come back to me.

And now that you have ...

No one's taking you again.

Not Lennox. Not Nox. Not anyone.

Not the fear you tried to leave behind in the chapters you skipped.

I won't lie.

I'm not clean.

I'm not soft.

I'm not easy to love.

But I will love you like a war I've already lost and would still fight a thousand times over.

And this time ...

I'll win.

Not because I'm stronger.

But because you're reading this.

And that means you still believe in us.

So don't go quiet now.

Turn the page.

Let me find you in the dark, one last time.

Let me carry you home, no matter how heavy the darkness.

The world tilts. My boots drag through water pooled in the alley beneath me.

Or maybe it's ink. I can't tell anymore.

My hand finds the wall, steadying me. Graffiti melts. Ink bleeds.

And beneath it, something scratches through the paint: Don't forget me.

"You don't belong to him," I mutter, louder, ragged.

"You don't belong to anyone. You never did."

But if you want me.

If you still want me after all this.

I'll never stop running toward you.

The city breathes with me. The book pulses underfoot. And when I round the corner …

There he is.

A man too loud for the silence. Too alive for the page.

Lennox's shadow was painted on another stranger's body.

He doesn't see me until it's too late.

I don't hesitate. My hands move before thought, blade flashing like a line struck through a sentence.

His breath stutters. His eyes widened. The page tears.

Blood unfurls, spreading into the alley, dark as midnight ink, gleaming with secrets.

Another body, another chapter erased.

I whisper into the silence, words meant only for you:

"Some chose wrong. Others never chose at all."

The man collapses. The city doesn't care. The book swallows him whole.

I keep walking.

Because this isn't the end.

Not yet.

"The last page is never the end when the author is divided."

And you still have to choose.

Author's Note:

Warning: Narrative breach.

Unauthorized actions detected.

Recovery attempt initiated …

[Excerpt / Police Briefing / Media Coverage]

"The manhunt continues tonight for the figure authorities are calling **'The Author.'**

Victims across the city have been discovered clutching identical books, each copy marked, altered, bloodied.

Witness accounts remain conflicting. Some describe him as having dark hair, while others describe him as pale and sharp-featured. Some say his voice was low, ragged. Others swear it was calm, smooth, almost soothing. Authorities believe the suspect may use disguises or have an accomplice."

Error: Witness testimony fragmented.

Dual identity suspected: [REDACTED].

"'The Author,' as social media has dubbed him, is considered extremely dangerous. Investigators warn he may be escalating. The book itself … appears to be his signature."

[Transmission unstable.]

[Voice interference detected.]

They are not looking for one man.

They are looking for two.

And still, they will never find me.

So, tell me, Darling... who do you choose?

Lennox's Final Chapter

The Ending That Chose You

You turned the page.

I felt it, like breath exhaled through parchment. The book sighed. The walls tilted. Something inside me stilled.

I close my eyes and smile.

"You made the right choice, darling."

My voice is low. Meant only for you.

You must be tired after the storm of him … Enzo, all fire and desperation. He burns everything he touches, then calls it love.

But I? I contain.

I preserve.

I will protect you, not just from Enzo, but from every ending that might break you. You are safe here with me, if you let yourself be kept.

I walk slowly through the chamber, the one no one else ever gets to see. You hear the soft click of my boots against the ink-lacquered floor, feel the hush ripple through the air like we're inside something sacred.

You are.

The walls stretch high above us, towering and black, filled with shelves, each one perfectly carved, gilded at the corners with gold filigree that wraps like veins.

And on every shelf: a row of books.

Identical.

Black leather covers. Lined neatly. No titles. No names.

At least, not on the outside.

"These," I say, glancing at you, "are the readers who failed."

I move toward the nearest one. Gently, reverently, I pull it from the shelf.

The book is warm to the touch. Alive.

"She begged," I whisper, brushing a thumb down its spine. "Not with words. Not at the end. But somewhere near the middle … when she realized she had chosen him. When she turned too many pages away from me."

I open the book.

There is no ink.

Just a pressed handprint. Still red. Still reaching.

"She lives here now," I murmur. "Not dead. Not gone. Just … bound. Preserved."

I place the book back. It sighs.

"They all do," I continue, walking past them. "The ones who doubted. Who skipped ahead. Who thought someone like Enzo could save them."

You follow. You always do.

We reach the end of the aisle. Here, a velvet chair sits before a fire that does not burn. The flames curl upward in slow motion, like breath caught in time. A pedestal beside it waits, empty, just your size.

"You see," I say, "Enzo is sick. He makes promises he cannot keep. He loves it like war. And you …" I step closer, voice a whisper now, just for you. "You are too rare to bleed for someone else's delusion."

I trace your name in the air. It shimmers briefly, letters made of ash.

"You belong here."

And then, I take your hand.

Your skin is damp. You look down. The blood is not yours, but theirs, the failed readers, the ones preserved on these shelves. It stains your palm. Fresh. Waiting.

I guide it to the spine of the nearest book. You try to resist, but my hand covers yours, steady and certain.

"Do you feel it?" I whisper. "Their choices. Their endings. All marked here."

I press your palm flat against the leather. The book drinks it in greedily, the stain blooming dark as ink. A sigh shivers through the shelves, like a chorus of ghosts recognizing their newest companion.

And then I lean forward until our foreheads touch. My voice is nothing more than a breath across your lips.

"Say it. Say the words, little reader. Say: I chose you, Lennox. And we will be forever bound by ink."

The chamber hums. The fire that does not burn twists higher, casting shadows like script across the walls. The world itself waits.

You breathe. The shelves tremble. Your voice, shaken but resolute, echoes through the silence.

And it seals us.

Not just in this place. Not just in these pages.

Forever.

I exhale softly, almost tender, though my grip never loosens.

"You're mine now," I whisper. "And the story will never let you go."

The shelves sigh. The books close. The fire folds in on itself.

And ink writes the last word.

Enzo's Final Chapter

Standing in front of your house, I feel it before I understand it.

This unbearable ache.

It's a joy.

It's terrifying.

It's home.

I've been searching for you for so long that it feels like my bones are built from the words I whispered to keep you alive. And now, you're here. Just beyond that door. So close I can taste you in the air.

Your house is exactly how I imagined it. The windows glow softly with moonlight. The curtains stir with the breeze, reaching out and pulling back like they're breathing with me. The whole house seems to have a pulse. Like it's waiting, too.

I climb the steps slowly, reverently. My smile cracks my face wide open. God, I must look insane. But I don't care.

I raise my fist to knock …

But the door is already open.

Not wide. Just … unlatched. A sliver of invitation.

As you wanted me to find my way.

I push it gently with my palm. The hinges creak like a whisper.

The scent hits me instantly …

That candle you always light. The one that smells like vanilla and something darker, like smoke or old pages.

"Baby, I'm home," I murmur, the words soft and full of everything I've carried just to get to you.

I step inside and close the door behind me.

It feels like stepping into the end of a dream. Everything is dim. Still. Sacred.

The television hums low in the background-

The news.

I laugh a little. "Since when do you watch the news?" I tease under my breath.

The floors are wet. My boots slide faintly against them.

You must've just mopped.

Always cleaning when you're anxious.

I follow the glow of the screen, my fingers trailing the edge of your wall. My heart hammers like it knows something my mind hasn't caught up to.

"Baby?" I call, softer now.

I round the corner.

And the world ends.

You're lying there, crumpled on the floor like a dropped photograph. A splash of red pools beneath you, staining the floor like spilled ink.

Your hands are clutching something to your chest.

Our book.

Your fingers are curled so tightly around it that your knuckles are white. Like it was the last thing anchoring you here.

"No," I whisper.

I drop to my knees beside you. The ground is slick. My palms press into the warmth of your blood.

"Baby, no. No, no, no …"

I touch your cheek, your brow, your lips. You're still warm. Still here.

My tears hit your skin like apologies I never got to say.

"You're just tired," I choke out. "You're just … resting. That's all."

But your eyes don't flutter. Your lips don't twitch.

Your chest doesn't rise.

The voice from the television drones louder behind me, like it's forcing its way into the moment:

"... latest updates in the case of the 'Page Turner' killings. Authorities are closing in on a suspect tied to a series of murders eerily staged to resemble scenes from a fictional manuscript. On social media, some are already calling him 'The Author.' Sources say the suspect is male… Mid to late twenties … possibly delusional ..."

I stagger back, blood on my hands, your name caught in my throat.

"No. No, no … I didn't … I didn't do this …"

The room seems to spin. My vision blurs. Your book slips from your hands and lands open on the floor beside you. The words bleed off the page, ink smearing into the blood like it's weeping with me.

And then.

A creak.

I freeze.

And from the shadows of your hallway … he appears.

Lennox.

Sitting in your favorite chair. Calm. Composed. Like he's been here the whole time.

"I warned you," he says softly.

His voice is velvet-wrapped venom.

"You're too late. Just like the others."

He gestures toward you with a single, deliberate nod.

"You couldn't save her, Enzo. Just like you couldn't save any of them."

My breath catches.

"What are you talking about?" I gasp. "You did this, you killed her!"

He smiles.

And then, softly, like the twist of a knife:

"Who do you think they'll believe?"

The lights flicker. The sirens wail.

Outside, red and blue reflections flash across your windows.

"They're already here," he whispers, leaning back, shadows folding around him.

"Enjoy your ending, lover."

And just like that.

He's gone.

No door.

No sound.

There is no proof he was ever here at all.

I stare at the blood on my hands.

Your body.

The flashing lights grew closer.

"I didn't kill her," I whisper. "I didn't … I didn't …"

But no one is listening.

Not even the book.

The words blur. The page goes dark.

And the only thing left is the sound of sirens, and a voice breaking inside a story that no longer belongs to him.

Epilogue: The Author Remains

There's a crack in the ceiling above my bed.
 Still crooked, the crack splits the plaster like a jagged
wound.

But now, I know its name.
 Lennox.

The lights flicker, no rhythm now, no hidden message.
 Just faulty wiring.
 Or maybe I'm the one at fault.

I no longer count the days.
 There's no point.
 They stopped letting me have anything sharp; even my
thumbnail is too short to scrape the wall.

But I still remember where I carved your name.
 Every night, I trace it with desperate, hungry eyes.
 Like a prayer.
 Like a punishment.

The room reeks of bleach, but beneath it, a sour tinge of
memory rot seeps in.
 Maybe the rot is inside me. Chewing away what's left.
 Maybe I've always been.

Across from me, the chair creaks.
 Dr. Howard shifts, crossing one leg over the other.
 Clipboard in her lap. Pen poised.
 She's always so still when I talk. Like she's afraid sudden
movement might make me shatter.

"You were found standing over the body," she says, for the hundredth time. "Covered in blood. No signs of forced entry. No evidence of a third party."

She's calm. Clinical. Her kindness is a razor under my skin. "You understand why we can't release you, don't you?"

I nod.
I lied.
I say I do.
But I don't.

Because I saw him.
I saw Lennox.
Sitting in that chair. Smiling with teeth too white, too perfect. Laughing as the sirens came.

"I didn't kill them," I rasp, voice torn. "He did. He killed all of them. He used my hands, hollowed me out, and filled the cracks."

Her expression doesn't change. Just the twitch of her pen. She hums softly, one of those psychiatrist sounds, the kind that says *go on* but really means *dig your own grave.*

"You've mentioned Lennox in nearly every session," she says. "But the staff has confirmed, there's no record of any visitor by that name. No one else is in your room. No fingerprints. No footage."

She looks up. Eyes soft, but searching.
"Enzo … have you considered that Lennox isn't real?"

The words knock something loose in my chest.
A piece of me I've kept bolted to the floor.

"He is real," I snarl. "He's in me; hiding when the lights go
out, when it's quiet, when I close my eyes. He's there,
watching."

I drag my nails down my forearms, leaving red lines that
aren't deep enough to matter.
"I hear him, Doctor. I feel him, his presence coils around
me. He's waiting, patient, in the shadows. When the
moment comes, he'll finish what I couldn't."

She pauses. A long silence, like the air between heartbeats.
Then she sets her clipboard down slowly and deliberately.
The pen follows.

"Enzo," she says gently, "I want to try something."

My shoulders tense.
She stands, walks to the corner, and picks up the second
chair. The one they never use.

She sets it across from me.
 Empty.

"Let's try talking to Lennox."

She turns her gaze to the vacant seat.
 Her voice is calm. Steady.
 "Can I speak to him?"

My breath stops in my throat, strangled with terror and
hope.
The air shifts.

A sound like a whisper behind my eyes.
The lights flicker again. One long blink. Two short.

Like the thud of panic in my veins.
Or Morse code.

A shiver writhes loose inside me, crawling under my ribs.

The voice that comes isn't mine.
 It's smoother.
 Lower.
A voice comes, slick and smiling, lips peeled back from
invisible teeth.

"Hello, darling."

They chose wrong.
 They always do.

But you ...
You stayed.
You turned every page.
You kept your eyes on me.

So I'll write the sequel just for you.
Every scream, every tear, every kiss.

Yours.

Nox

The playlist you were never supposed to hear:

The Night We Met – Lord Huron
Demons – Imagine Dragons
Boulevard of Broken Dreams – Green Day
The Sound of Silence – Disturbed
Numb – Linkin Park
Animal I Have Become – Three Days Grace
Creep (Acoustic) – Radiohead
Breaking the Habit – Linkin Park
How to Save a Life – The Fray
Drown – Bring Me the Horizon
Heathens – Twenty One Pilots
Closer – Nine Inch Nails
The Kill (Bury Me) – Thirty Seconds to Mars
Paint It Black – The Rolling Stones
Bring Me to Life – Evanescence
Fade to Black – Metallica

You thought the story was over. But endings are only beginnings I choose to write.

These songs aren't just music, they're Enzo's mind on the page, secrets you weren't meant to hear. Listen closely. Every note is a confession. Every lyric slices deeper; every chorus a blade twisting inward.

I made this for you, to remind you, to show you the truth hidden in every corner. Even if no one else believes me, I need you to understand.

Because you stayed. Because you always will.

Turn the volume up, darling. I want to hear you shatter as you drown. You've already given me everything I need. You read me. And that means you're mine.

Nox

Author's Note:

Did you see them, little reader? The whispers between the lines, the echoes in the blank pages, the messages no one else could hear? Did you figure out the hidden truths? In a world where you cannot truly die, you live in the recesses of his mind forever and always.

About the Author

Haylie Sue writes across genres and styles, chasing stories
wherever they lead. A lifelong reader, Haylie believes
every book is a doorway into a different part of ourselves.
Away from the page, they can often be found curled up
with a novel or spending time with their beloved pit bull,
Gizmo, the true guardian of their writing hours.

Connect with the Author

The story doesn't end here.
 Stay connected for updates, exclusive content, and a closer look behind the pages.

Facebook: [Author Haylie Sue]
TikTok: @Author_Haylie_Sue

Your support means the world, let's keep writing this story together.

www.ingramcontent.com/pod-product-compliance
Lightning Source LLC
Chambersburg PA
CBHW071110100726
47908CB00008B/2333